Trudy

Chapter one

The young girl lay cold and hungry on the cold floor of an old abandon trailer. She had been laying in her own urine and feces for days. She was hand-cuffed to a rail and could not break free. She flinched every time she heard a noise hoping it was someone coming to free her but scared it was her captor coming to rape her.

At first the man who did this to her would come once every day but he hadn't showed up for the last few days. He hadn't raped her since the first day but every time he returned she feared it would happen again. He left her with a box of crackers and a gallon jug of water. She ate all of the crackers and the gallon jug of water was almost gone.

She worried that if he didn't return she would starve to death but at the same time she would rather starve to death than be raped again. She screamed as loud as she could several times a day at first hoping someone would hear her but now she didn't even have the strength to scream or even try any more.

Fifty miles away, Nick had just walked in the door from a hard day at work and before he even closed the door, his wife Erica started yelling orders to him from down the hall. "Stir the spaghetti on the stove and take the bread out of the oven."

She was in the bathroom putting on some mascara and putting her hair back to get ready to go to work. She worked nights at the hospital as a nurse's aide and Nick worked days in construction. They didn't have much time together and it was taking a toll on their marriage.

Nick took the bread out of the oven and was stirring the spaghetti when Erica came into the kitchen and started setting the table and pouring them both a glass of sweet tea. "Dang I have to eat fast, I am running late." Erica looked at her watch as she scarfed her food down.

"Why don't you get your make up on and your hair fixed a little bit earlier instead of waiting till the last minute every day?" Nick asked as he buttered his bread.

"Don't even start with me Nick; I don't have time to argue. When I got up today I had to wash your breakfast dishes and do the laundry and write out all of the bills. I have been busy ever since I got out of bed." She pushed her plate away and started putting on her shoes.

"My breakfast dishes were a bowl and spoon and coffee cup. I had cereal." Nick yelled back.

"I said I don't have time to argue, I got to go. But you have free time every evening and you go to the bar or go watch sports at your friend's house and all of my free time I am cleaning or cooking or doing laundry."

Before Nick could respond Erica slammed the door and went off to work. On her way to work she said a prayer for God to please help her to not be so grouchy and for her and Nick to work everything out.

With them both working different shifts the only time they had together was a little time when Nick got home from work and Before Erica had to leave. Sometimes Nick would get off work a little late and they would only have a few minutes. Then when they did sit down to share a meal it was rushed because she would have to leave for work. The lack of time together was causing problems in their marriage. They had the weekends but on Friday night Erica would get home at 4:30 am. She would eat a snack and maybe get on Facebook to unwind and then Nick would get up about 5:30 but he is like a zombie when he wakes up. He doesn't like to talk until after he drinks some coffee. So by the time he was awake enough to talk it would be time for Erica to go to bed and sleep half the day. So basically they had Saturday evening and Sunday together and Erica had to work one Sunday a month.

When Erica and Nick first got married Erica thought she found the

A

perfect man. They got along so well and spent all of their time together. Erica only worked part time as a server at a seafood restaurant back then and she only worked lunch shifts through the week. Nick and the guys he worked with would come in the restaurant for lunch a couple times a week because she could give them free soda and tea. So they were together all the time. In the evenings they would go for walks. The apartment complex they lived in had a gym and a pool. So they worked out together a couple times a week and in the summer they would spend a lot of evenings swimming in the pool. Then they decided to buy a house and start a family and they realized she would need to make more money. She went to night school and took a few classes and then got a full time job at the hospital as a nurse aide. She had to work evenings but the couple thought it would be perfect for when they had kids because then they wouldn't have to pay a baby sitter because one of them would always be at home.

So they bought a cute little ranch house with a great back yard for kids and hoped that in the next year or so Erica would get pregnant. Erica always had very bad minstrel cramps and was diagnosed with mild endometriosis. The doctor said she might have a hard time getting pregnant but her case was mild and no treatment was necessary. A few years went by and she was still not pregnant so she went to see a fertility doctor. Her endometriosis had gotten much worse and he said she may eventually need surgery. He told her that she may never be able to have kids. She was already almost 35 years old so it didn't look good.

Erica was devastated, all her dreams of her and Nick having little kids that looked like them were gone. They both were very good looking. Erica was tall and slender with long dark hair and brown eyes. She usually dressed like a hippy at home, a lot of tie died shirts and pants with wild prints on them but to work she had to wear scrubs. She didn't wear much makeup only a little eye liner and mascara. At home she wore her hair down with a headband but to work she put it in a ponytail. Nick was very tall, dark hair always tan and muscular from working outside in construction.

Erica started looking into adoption but every time she tried to talk to

A

Nick about it he would say he thought their lives were so hectic right now and money is tight, maybe we should wait. Then she would say we aren't getting any younger and he would say we will have a serious talk about it when we have more time. They kept saying we need to sit down and have a serious discussion about it but they just never had the time. Before they knew it they both turned 40 years old and still never seriously checked into adoption.

With them both being on different work schedules they just didn't do the fun things together like they did when they first got married and lived in the apartment. Erica went out with the girls from work every now and then but other than that she didn't have much of a social life. The house, cooking, grocery shopping laundry took most of her time so she started thinking how would I ever have time for a kid anyway. Nick started hanging out with some of his single guy friends in the evening at a local bar watching sports on the television. That caused a lot of arguing because it was costing money and she felt like it was not fair because she didn't seem to have time to do anything fun.

So as much as she loved her job and her coworkers she stated looking for a day job so that her and Nick would be on the same schedule. The hospital didn't have any day positions available but she found the job ad for a nurse aide at Sunset Care Center. It was like the nicest nursing home in southeast Missouri and most of the residents were rich people. The pay was actually a little more than she was making at the hospital. She went for the first interview and they said she had more experience than all of the other applicants.

Then she had to go for a second interview with the director of the care center. The director told Erica that they were looking for someone who could work 6 am till 3 pm and that she would have ten ladies' to look after and basically just watch them all day and take care of their needs.

"We need someone for section C witch is in our assisted living area. All ten lady's in section C are in pretty good health and don't need a lot of assistance. Here at Sunset we want everyone to be treated special. The

A

residents and their family's pay a lot more money to be here rather than some of the other Care Centers because of all of the individual attention."

Erica sat quietly listening and wondering if this meant that she got the job.

"We have nurses, occupational and physical therapist checking on them and working with them regularly. We have an excellent cleaning crew that takes care of bed sheets and regular cleaning. All we will want you to focus on is making sure they get down to the café for their meals or if they want to eat in their rooms you will need to bring them a tray."

"Also we have a game room, a lounge, a library; exercise classes all kinds of activities. Part of your job will be to encourage them to take part in activities or to mingle with the other residents. When their family's come to visit we want them to hear that their loved one is having a great time and has lots of friends here."

"Every resident has a large room kind of like a studio apartment. They have a bed and a small living room area and a little kitchen area with a kitchen table. No stove or refrigerator, just a small counter where they can have a coffee pot or microwave if they want one."

Erica said, "It sounds great, I think I will like working here and the hours are perfect for me."

Then the director told her that she would have to work weekends and that her days off would be Monday and Tuesday.

"Oh No, that won't work, I am only looking for a new job so I will be on the same schedule as my husband" Erica said disappointedly.

So she decided to tell them no thanks. She went home and started checking the internet for other job opportunity's when her phone rang. It was the director of Sunset Care Center, and she offered Erica the job with weekends off and more pay.

"You are more qualified than anyone else that has applied for this

A

position. I really think you would be a great fit for the women in section C of Sunset Care Center. I really hope you will accept my offer." The director told her to think about it and then she hung up the phone.

Erica really didn't need to think about it. The hours will be perfect and now that she offered even more pay she definitely wanted the job. She really didn't know if she would like the job but because of the hours and the pay she called the director right back and told her she would put her two week notice in at her other job. In her mind she was thinking I'm probably not going to like it as much as my job I have now but I love my husband and want to work on my marriage so I might hate this job but it is what I have to do.

Nick was really happy when he heard no weekends and also more money. She put her two week notice in at the hospital and on her last Friday all the gal's had a big party for her. She promised them that she would come in and visit sometime and bring them all donuts.

A

Chapter Two

Erica started her new job the next Monday. It was hard to change her sleep pattern so the first few nights she didn't get much sleep, but she knew this was going to be great for their marriage. We would both be going to bed at the same time so it would definitely help our sex life and we would both be getting up early in the morning and we would have our evenings together, I am doing the right thing she thought to herself.

The first morning she hadn't slept very well at all, partly because she wasn't use to sleeping at night and partly because she wasn't use to having Nick in bed with her. He took up the whole bed and he snored. She told herself it would just take some getting used to. The alarm went off at 5:00 am and they both rushed around to get ready. Nick packed his cooler and ate a bowl of cereal. Erica was glad that she didn't need new cloths or anything. She was still going to be wearing scrubs and putting her hair back in a ponytail. She threw on a little mascara and put her hair back and joined Nick in the kitchen for a bowl of fruit loops. He said, "This is going to be nice eating breakfast together."

She told him, "maybe when I get use to sleeping at night and I get a good night sleep, maybe I'll even cook you breakfast every once in a while."

As she started to head out the door he came over and gave her a big hug and said, "I hope you love your new job and I hope the people you work with are as great as your old coworkers." At that moment she knew for sure she was doing the right thing. But she had no idea how much this decision was going to change her life.

She loved Nick so much and she really wanted their marriage to be better, the way it was when they first got married and lived in the apartment. Back then they always had time together to do fun things. On her drive to Sunset Care Center she thought about having the time to finally have that talk about adopting. She wondered if she was crazy to even think about that at age 40. But she knew at least now Nick and I will

A

get a chance to talk about it.

She arrived at work about ten minute's early kind of dreading even going in. She was so comfortable at her old job. She wasn't looking forward to being the new person. As she walked from the staff parking lot to the building she said a quick prayer. Erica walked in and told the receptionist who she was and the receptionist introduced her to an elderly lady named Pam. Pam was retiring and Erica would be taking her position. She was going to spend a week training her.

Pam showed her where to put her purse and jacket and took her to a little cafe area. Cooks and servers were busy getting tables and food ready for breakfast. It smelled so good.

Pam and Erica sat at a table in the corner so they wouldn't be in the way. "I will show you all around the whole place after we get everyone to breakfast. You are going to be responsible for all of the residents in section C. In section C there are ten ladies. Every morning when you get here you need to make sure that they are up and dressed. They cannot come to the café in their pajamas. They will either go to this cafe area for breakfast or they will want breakfast in their room. Most of our ladies are in pretty good shape and want to go to the cafe for all of their meals except for Trudy she is in room 10 and she always eats in her room."

Erica asked if she was in poor health and Pam told her, no she is about 80 years old and in pretty good health. She is just a rich snob. Come on lets go meat the gal's.

The first one of the residents that Erica met was in room one. She was an awesome woman named Julie. She was almost 90 and she had long hair all twisted up on her head. She had turquoise rings on all of her fingers. She was full of energy and she gave Erica a hug and said "Do you like to sing karaoke? This is the karaoke Christmas lounge." She had her room decorated like Christmas even though it was not anywhere near Christmas time." Erica didn't know what to think, but she knew she was going to like this gal.

A

"I have an awful voice so I have never even tried to sing karaoke." Erica laughed.

Julie chuckled "well that's going to change sister, it don't matter how you sound we do it for fun and you are going to love it."

She showed Erica her karaoke machine and she had hundreds of CDs. Pam said to Julie, "You can show her your stuff and get to know her later, let's go get breakfast." and they all walked to the cafe. She didn't need any help she walked just fine. She didn't even use a walker.

Erica met the lady's in room 2 3 4 5 and 6 and helped them to get dressed and walked them to the cafe. Most of them got around just fine but a few of them used walkers but did very well. The lady in room two was the only one who had trouble getting around. The lady's in rooms 7 8 and 9 were a little younger and were already up and dressed and sitting on Bettys bed talking about a nice looking new man who just joined the Care Center yesterday. When Pam and Erica walked in the room they didn't hear them. They are younger than the rest but all three of them are hard of hearing.

Pam yelled lady's this is Miss Erica. She is going to be my replacement. They were all happy to meet Erica and gave her hugs. They all looked to be about 75 or 80 or so and they were super friendly. Betty said, my name is Betty this is my room and this is Clair and Rose they are in 8 and 9. We call ourselves the golden girls. Then they all laughed. Pam said, "Come on golden girls, breakfast is getting cold". So they walked with them down to the cafe. They all three got around good and didn't need much help at all. Pam said to Erica, "The three of them are trouble. They keep me on my toes. They are always over in section A and B flirting with all the men. You will have to keep your eye on them."

After the golden girls took their seats, Pam said, "Now we need to take Trudy her food." Erica followed Pam into the kitchen where the cooks had trays all ready for the aids to take to the people who wanted to eat in their room. As they walked down the hall with a Tray for Trudy, Pam told

A

Erica that Trudy was filthy rich and she thinks she is better than everyone and too good to eat with them.

When they entered her room there sat a beautiful women sitting in her chair reading a book. Her room was much fancier than all the other rooms. She had a canopy bed with beautiful violet expensive looking bed sheets and blankets. The furniture in the room was super fancy and expensive looking. Trudy had Cole black perfectly fixed hair. She was sitting in her plush chair in a silk robe.

Pam said "Good morning Trudy we have your breakfast. This is Miss Erica she will be taking my place next week." Trudy didn't even look up from her book. She put her hand up in the air as if to say don't bother me. Then she told them to set the tray on the table. "I am reading."

Pam said, "I wanted to introduce you to Miss Erica who will be taking my place."

Trudy said, "I just told you I am reading right now."

They left the room and Pam said "What did I tell you. She is a snob."

Erica asked "What is her problem?"

Pam told Erica that her and her husband owned an investment company and that it did very well and she lived in a mansion up near St Louis. Her husband died about 5 years ago and her son put her in the Care Center about a year ago. Her son is a doctor at one of the hospitals in Cape Girardeau, he said he wanted her closer to him and this is one of the best nursing homes in Missouri, so he brought her here. She was not happy about it. She didn't want to sell her house but her son said that she wasn't of sound mind to make her own decisions and with so much money at stake he became her power of attorney and she is bitter.

Erica asked, "Does her son come and spend a lot of time with her?"

Pam replied "No he usually only comes for holidays and that is about it. He takes good care of her though. She has a personal beautician who

A

comes once a week and does her hair. Someone comes once a week and does her nails and pedicure. And her favorite chefs from St Louis cook her meals and send them all the way down here to her twice a week. She gets her special meal on Wednesday at lunch so on Wednesday noon don't bring her a tray. The other special meal comes on the weekend you won't be here so you only need to remember Wednesday lunch."

Pam and Erica talked as they headed back to the cafe to check on their girls.

As they got close to the cafe they could her Julie, She was standing on her chair banging a spoon on her plate, yelling listen up everyone. Pam grabbed her and scolded, "Miss Julie you get down from there."

Julie said, "I need to get everyone's attention." Then she yelled, "Listen up people." Then she whistled loud and said, "We all need to make sure we tell the cooks and service staff thank you because that was a great breakfast. So before everyone goes back to their rooms let's give them a hand."

Everyone started clapping all around the room. Erica heard Betty say to Rose, "What are we clapping for?" Rose said, "I didn't hear what they said but I guess we are clapping because Julie got down off the chair."

They got everyone back to their rooms and then Pam and Erica got to sit down and eat a little breakfast. They sat in the cafe and ate Biscuits and gravy. The food was really high quality good food and Erica was surprised that she gets to eat here for free. That was a perk she didn't even know about.

Pam showed Erica around the whole building and it was very nice. Erica was thinking to herself this is the nicest nursing home I have ever seen and she realized she was very lucky to get this job even though she missed the girls from the hospital.

"Sections A B C and D are all the assisted living part of the Care Center. A and B are men and C and D are women except in section D there

A

are two married couples." Pam explained and then she showed her the exercise, game room, library and sitting area.

Erica was very impressed at how nice everything was, "I want to live here! How old do you have to be?" Erica laughed.

Pam chuckled, "No kidding, these ladies have it made."

After she showed her around the nursing home part of the Care Center, they went back to check on all the girls in section C. Most of them were taking naps. Betty, Rose and Clair were in Julie's room singing and it sounded like they were all having a ball. So they went down to room 10 to check on Trudy. She was asleep in her chair and she hadn't touched her breakfast.

Pam said, "Just let her sleep. She doesn't like people to tell her what to do."

The day was going by fast. Pam showed Erica where the schedule for activity's and exercise classes that Sunset offers is. She told her none of her lady's ever wants to exercise but management keeps telling her to try to push them to come.

"They say it would be good for them but if they don't want to exercise you can't make them."

"I agree with management, they are so lucky to have that offered to them; I wish they would take advantage of it." Erica said, thinking about how much she missed her gym that they had at the apartment.

Pam rolled her eyes, "Trust me, these old gal's don't want to exercise so don't waste your breath trying to get them to do it. I have tried."

"Some of them will go to the library and you can't keep the golden girls out of the men's lounge." Pam said as they passed by the men's lounge and there in the lounge with the men where all three golden girls.

Pam pointed her finger at them and said, "You gal's better behave

A

yourselves."

As they walked back to section C, Pam told Erica, "It's a pretty easy job you don't have to do much because most of them take pretty good care of them self. The evening staff gives showers so you won't ever have to worry about that. Every day one or two of them will have an accident in their pants but most of the time they take care of it them self."

The day went by pretty fast. All and all it was a pretty good day.

Chapter Three

Erica got home from work before Nick and she was able to get a shower, do a load of laundry, straighten up the house and have dinner started before he got home. He walked in the door and saw her cooking dinner and the house all cleaned up and he said, "I think I'm going to like this. How was your first day?" **B**ut before he could finish the sentence she started telling him all about her day. They got to sit down and enjoy dinner without Erica having to gobble hers down and head out the door. After Nick took his shower they watched a little TV. The new job was working out just fine.

On Friday the cooking staff made a 'going away' cake for Pam and all the resident's presented her with a book in which they all wrote a page telling her how much they will miss her and about their favorite memory's with her. It was very nice. After the little party they took Trudy a piece of cake because she didn't come to the going away party. Her beautician was in the room dyeing her hair.

Pam said, "I just wanted to tell you good bye and I am leaving you in good hands. Miss Erica will take good care of you."

Trudy replied, "I wrote in your book."

Pam and Erica went down to the lounge to look in her book and see what Trudy and all the others wrote. All of the residents wrote very nice things about their good times with Pam. The last page was Trudy's. It was a very nice page. She had taped a picture of herself on the page and wrote I hope you never forget me and I hope you have a wonderful retirement. Then she told of some of the great trips her and her late husband went on when they retired and about how much fun and how wonderful the years right after retiring were and she said don't let them pass you by, enjoy.

As Pam and Erica were walking down the hall to leave for the day, Rose came sprinting past them mumbling, "I pooped my pants."

A

"Should I go help her?" Erica asked Pam.

"She will take care of it herself. She wears pull ups and she has a big supply of wet wipes in her bathroom. The only one who sometimes needs help cleaning her butt is Ada in room 2 and once in a while Page in room 3. They will let you know if they need help."

As they walked to their cars Erica thanked Pam for all of her help and wished her a happy retirement. Pam gave Erica her phone number and said if she had any questions she could call her. Erica got in her car feeling very confident and happy about her new job.

Every night Nick would have to hear about all of these old lady's but he was happy that Erica liked her job and it was nice having time together. They were still trying to adjust to the new schedule, even though it was great having time together they were used to having the whole bed to their selves and Nicks friends were bugging him to come down to the bar. He did go one night and came home late and drunk and Erica gave him a hard time because she switched jobs for them to have their evenings together and she didn't like him drinking and driving. Also money was tight and it's a waste of money. They got into a big argument.

"First of all it's less than a mile away and secondly I am not drunk, I had 5 beers. And anyway if I hadn't gone to hang out with the guy's I would have just watched TV and you would have just been laying on the couch half asleep, so what difference does it make?" Nick yelled down the hall way as he went to go brush his teeth and climb into bed.

Erica yelled, "You probably spent 25 or 30 dollars and we could have both went to dinner or did something together with that money, we never have a date. We just sit here and watch stupid stuff that you put on the TV, it's boring and I fall asleep on the couch. This, by the way is where I am going to sleep tonight."

Nick went to bed and Erica lay down on the couch and pulled the afghan up over her shoulders. She didn't feel very comfortable but she figured that Nick would come down the hall any minute and apologize but he

A

never did and she finally fell asleep on the couch.

Erica woke up to the sound of Nick making coffee in the kitchen; she pulled the little afghan she was cuddling up with over her head. She heard Nick come in the living room and sit in his recliner and start sipping coffee. She just laid there and tried to get back to sleep. After Nick went to the kitchen for more coffee he came back to the living room set his coffee on the coffee table and sat on the edge of the couch and started to rub her back.

"Hey I don't want to fight with you." Nick said, as he picked up his coffee cup.

Erica pulled the afghan off her head and told him she didn't want to fight either, but she was lonely all the time when they worked different shifts and now they are on the same schedule, but she still feels lonely. "Maybe if we adopted a child I wouldn't ever feel lonely. Maybe that is what's missing."

Nick asked "Do you really still want to do that at our age. I am almost 41. By the time we go through the adoption process I will be 42. I don't know if I have patience for a baby anymore, how about we get a puppy?"

Erica pulled the afghan back over her head.

Nick said "If you really want a baby then go for It." and he picked up his coffee cup and headed down the hall to the bathroom.

Erica got up and got herself a cup of orange juice and went down the hall and knocked on the bathroom door. "I'm taking a shit." was the reply.

She stood at the door and said "I don't want a baby unless you want it too."

She heard the toilet flush and the sink water come on and the sound of the soap dispenser being pumped like ten times. He always waist's soap, he should do the shopping and see how much that stuff cost, she thought. Then the door opened and Nick gave her a big hug. "Let's go on a date this

A

weekend, and talk about our future." Nick said as he gave her a big squeeze. That is exactly what Erica wanted to hear.

Chapter four

Almost every morning after breakfast the golden girls would sing karaoke in Julie's room. Erica joined them most mornings. Julie had about every song you could think of and if she didn't have the song that you wanted, she would have her daughter download it. Julie's daughter Jesse would come visit her 3 or 4 times a week. She was a professor at the university and you could really tell she loved her mom.

After lunch everyday Erica would have to go searching for the golden girls because they were always over in section A because that is where all the hot men were. (That's what Ruth would say) One time she found Ruth in bed with the new guy. They had their cloths on and everything but they were lying in bed making out like a couple of teenagers. Julie never went over to section A with the golden girls because she said that she wasn't interested in any man. She would talk about her late husband Larry with a gleam in her eye. He was the love of her life and nobody could ever replace him.

Erica really loved her new job and she would come home every night and tell Nick about Julie wearing only a teddy, standing on her bed singing girls just one to have fun or the golden girl's sneaking around in section A. Nick would act like he was listening but he didn't talk much. Erica sometimes wondered if he wished she still worked nights. Sometimes she felt like she was getting on his nerves.

They started going on a date every Saturday night usually just out for ice cream or a taco, but they never did make a decision on adopting. Nick told Erica if a baby is what she really wants, she should start checking into how much it would cost and start getting the ball rolling before they get any older. She did do a little research on the subject but never did get started on the paper work because she felt like it wasn't really what Nick wanted.

Nick still went to the bar to hang with his guy friends sometimes but not as much as he used to. One week he went 2 nights in a row and then when he wanted to go out again the next night, Erica was not happy about it. She told him she was hoping they could talk because he was gone the last two nights.

She said "We never talk."

He said, "You talk nonstop. What do you want from me?"

Erica argued, "Yah, I talk and you don't even listen."

Then she found out he does listen because he repeated everything she had ever told him about the lady's at work.

He said, "I know all about Julie and her karaoke Christmas lounge and the golden girls hanging out with the guys."

And then he said, "You never give me a chance to say anything but if you want to know what I think, I'll tell you. I think you have favorites at that nursing home and you give them all of your attention and you aren't doing your job. They are paying you good money just to keep an eye on 10 ladies and to make sure all of their needs are met. Not just to visit and sing with the ones that you like." Then he went out the door.

At first she was so mad she threw her cup at the door and broke it and scratched the wood floor then cut herself cleaning it up. But later as she was soaking in the bath tub, she thought about what Nick said and she thought maybe he was right. I spend a lot of time in Julie's room singing and a lot of time with the golden girls. They are paying me to make sure all ten of them are happy and I am not doing a good job. She decided that starting tomorrow she was going to try to give all of the women more attention and even try to get to know Trudy.

The next day at work after everyone was taken to the cafe for their breakfast, Erica took Trudy her tray of breakfast like she did every morning but she brought herself a muffin to eat with Trudy. Trudy was up and in the rest room. When Trudy came out of the rest room, Erica had

A

her breakfast on the table and had them both a cup of coffee and a muffin for herself.

"Good morning Trudy. I hope you don't mind if I join you for breakfast. I brought myself a muffin in here to eat with you because I'm tired of eating in the cafe." Erica said with a big smile on her face, trying to look friendly.

Trudy said, "That is fine." She sat down and started to eat.

Erica asked her why she doesn't like eating at the cafe and she said, "I don't like eating with a bunch of strangers."

"You should try to get to know some of the lady's; they can be a lot of fun."

Trudy took a bite of her muffin and mumbled something.

Erica asked, "Have you ever sung karaoke?"

Trudy looked up and said, "I love to sing. When I was a teenager I was a singer in a band. We played at weddings and other events.

"I would love to hear you, maybe sometime you can go down to Julie's room and sing for us."

Trudy didn't say NO like Erica thought she would say. She said maybe and that was a good start. Then Erica asked her, "How about you tell me about your son, I would like to get to know you better Miss Trudy."

Trudy answered, "Not much to tell."

"I heard he was a doctor is that true?

"Yes he is very busy."

Then her stylist walked in and Erica remembered it was Friday time to get her hair done. As she left the room she felt good about how it went. She headed back to the cafe to get the lady's back to their rooms. The

A

golden girls were going to the lounge in section A to play cards with the guys. Julie had already gone back to her room, she peeked in on her she was just getting ready to watch a Johnny Depp movie her daughter brought her the night before.

Ada, the women in room 2 wasn't feeling well so Erica wheeled her down to see the nurse. The nurse said that she may have a stomach flu that was going around and to make sure to check her temp regularly and let her know if it goes up. Right when they got back to the room she threw up. After Erica got her cleaned up she got her in bed, took her temp, it was normal so she sat by the bed and asked her about her children. She told Erica that she had 6 kids. Erica had met a few of them but for the next hour she sat and listened to her tell about each one of her kids and grandkids with so much joy in her voice.

"I hope I'm not boring you?"

Erica rubbed Ada's arm, "No, of course not. I am enjoying hearing about your family. It sounds like you are all so close."

Then Ada said, "thank you, I think I am feeling a lot better now." Erica took her temp again and it was normal so she told her to get some rest and went to check on Miss Page the women in room 3.

As she walked next door she thought "Nick was right, I have been doing a crappy job, I'm so glad he brought it to my attention."

"Hi Miss Page, how are you today?" She had never seen anyone visit her, so she didn't even know if she had children.

She was lying in bed watching a game show. Without even looking up she said fine, in a drab voice. Erica sat down in the chair next to the bed and asked," how about if you tell me a little about yourself. I have been working here for a while now and I don't know anything about you."

Page asked still staring at the TV, "What do you want to know?"

Well, were you ever married?

A

Page answered, "Yes but my husband died when we were only married for 6 years."

"Oh I'm so sorry to hear that, and you never remarried?" she moved her chair a little closer.

"No, I was busy raising my son, he was my life." Page replied. Then she picked up the remote and turned off the game show and looked over at Erica with a sad look in her eye.

"Oh I don't think I have ever met your son."

Tears started to fill Page's eyes and she said, "My son took his own life when he was 21."

Erica didn't know what to say," Oh my goodness Miss Page I am so sorry."

She proceeded to tell Erica that her son had gotten married at age 20 and that she was so happy because he was depressed most of his teenage years and she was hoping his new bride would be all he needed to be happy and have a good life. His new bride found herself a boyfriend and my son shot himself in the head. She wept like it just happened even though it was over 40 years ago. Erica hugged her and sat on the side of her bed and talked with her until it was time to go down for lunch. Page said that she really didn't feel like eating but Erica told her it will make you feel better. So Page agreed to go to lunch. Erica walked her down to the café.

Ada didn't feel up to going to lunch and so she went back to visit the nurse. She never did have a fever but she still didn't feel good that afternoon.

Erica had to go search for the golden girls and tell them it was time for lunch. Spending more time with each one of the lady's made the day a little more hectic than usual but as she walked to her car that afternoon she really felt good about how the day went.

A

When Nick got home that night he apologized for going to the bar the night before. He said I know you wanted to talk and I just left and I'm sorry. They hugged and she told him that she really wants to work on their marriage.

"We have time together now, let's find a way to spend it together that we both enjoy."

They talked about maybe joining a bowling league or a gym. Erica told him that what he said last night was really helpful and she told him about her day. For once it seemed like he was listening. They had a great evening.

Chapter five

Over the next few months Erica spent as much time with Trudy as she would allow. Sometimes when she entered the room she would put up her hand and say I am reading, other times she would say I want to be alone and then Fridays her beautician would come and on Mondays she had her nails done. Erica still never met her son. Trudy would talk about him like she was proud and that he was very smart and successful but at the same time she would sometimes say her husband really wanted him to run their financial business so he could retire but that Michael the son wanted to go to med school and have nothing to do with our family business. When her husband did finally retire they sold the financial empire they had and invested the money. She said her and Bob her husband traveled and had the best time and always had plenty of money but she said if our son would have taken over our business by now we would be so rich. Erica told her "you are rich."

Trudy said, "I mean really rich."

"You can't take it with you and you live comfortably here and your son is happy with his life right."

She shrugged her shoulders and said," I don't know I don't see him much. You would think his kids would come see their grandma every once in a while but they are spoiled brats who only care about money and their self. My grandkids don't even bring their kids to come see me. My great grandkids don't even know me. When I had my own house and money they would come see me all the time and ask for money and I always gave it to them, like you said you can't take it with you. but then my son Michael decided that I was too old and he was worried someone was going to take advantage of my old age and swindle my money from me so I put him in charge of it all and next thing you know my house is up for sale and I am moving in here against my will. And now that I can't give away money nobody comes to see me. It doesn't surprise me that they don't come see their old granny now that I can't give them anything. The only one who surprises me is little Winnie. She is the only one of the

A

whole bunch who would come spend time with me and not ask for money. But I guess I was wrong about her because she came to see me a few times after I moved here and then never came back. I guess she only wanted money too."

"So you only have one son." Erica questioned.

"Yes Michael is my only son and he has three boys. The oldest, John is 52 years old, and he has two children and Steve is almost 50 and he has two children also. Then the youngest is Bill and he has one daughter and that is little Winnie."

Erica tried to think of something positive to say to Trudy. "Well how old is Winnie? Maybe she is just busy."

Trudy said "She is only 20 years old. When she came to see me here a couple of months ago she told me that she dropped out of college. She said she was scared to tell her dad but that college just wasn't for her."

Trudy went on to say that she thought Winnie was telling her about dropping out of college so that maybe she would tell her dad for her but now that she never came back to visit she guessed that Winnie was probably wanting money and found out that old granny didn't have any.

"Now come on Miss Trudy, just because she hasn't been here to visit doesn't mean all she wants is money. She probably got a job and hasn't had the time to come back. Did you ever tell her dad about her dropping out of college?"

"No, how could I? Billy never comes to see me. He doesn't even call. Michael hasn't been here in months. Michael calls once a week or so but we haven't talked about Winnie."

Erica tried again to make Trudy feel better. She said, "Think back to how busy you were when you were working. Life can get pretty hectic. I'm sure they all love you and wish they had more time to come visit."

'I suppose you are right. "Trudy said with her head down.

A

Erica tried to lift Trudy's spirits. "I wish you would get to know the other gal's. You could have a lot of fun with them. I am trying to get some of the others to go to an exercise class. Would you be interested in water aerobics or yoga?"

Trudy laughed, "I haven't exercised in years."

"You still look like you are in good shape. I bet you would like it if you gave it a try and I still want to hear you sing sometime soon." Erica told her to think about it as she left the room.

Erica was glad that Nick brought it to her attention that she wasn't doing her job if she didn't give equal attention to all of the ladies. It only took a little effort on her part and they all started opening up to her. And it seemed that some of them really needed someone to talk to.

One day when Erica was eating her morning muffin in Trudy's room, Trudy said, "Miss Erica I have a secret and I am thinking about telling you but I don't know if I should."

Erica put her muffin down and asked, "What is it, what kind of secret?"

"Well, I am not sure if I should tell you I need to get to know you better." So over the next few weeks they talked a lot about Erica's life. She told her about Nick and about her old job and how she switched jobs to have more time with her husband. She told her about not being able to have a baby and that her and Nick never got around to adopting and now she wonders if she is too old. Erica told Trudy about Nick going to the bar and about how it makes her mad and that they are starting to go on dates but they need a hobby or something to do to make life more fun on the weekends. Trudy told her the next time Nick goes to the bar you should go to the hospital and see the gal's that you use to work with.

Erica thought that was a great idea. "I should do that. I sometime just wish that I was able to have kids."

A

Trudy hit Erica in the arm and said "kid's aren't all they are cracked up to be. All they want is money."

Erica laughed, "well they wouldn't get much from me."

Nick and Erica never did join a bowling league but they continued to have a date night every Saturday. Sometimes they would go to 5:00 church and then out to dinner. Going to church was helping them to get along better. Sometimes they would go bowling. One Saturday night they went to a show and after words they went out for ice cream. They were sitting at a picnic table eating ice cream and they talked about if they were too old to adopt a child and if it was even still what they wanted to do. Nick said, "Kids are expensive and we struggle to pay our bills now, heck you yell at me for spending 20 bucks on beer when I go to the bar and I haven't even gone out with the guys because I know you will get mad if I spend money."

They didn't come to a decision but at least they were talking about it. Nick hadn't gone to the bar with his buds in a while not just because of money but also because he didn't want Erica throwing cups and cutting herself. So that night, while they were eating ice cream Erica told him what Trudy suggested about her going to see her friends from her old job. So they decided that next time there is a ball game he wants to see he can go to the bar and she won't complain, she will go see her old buds at the hospital and bring them donuts. Nick said ok but you have to buy day old donuts to save money and Erica said ok but you can only drink 2 beers. He said, "It's a deal."

A

Chapter six

Erica was really starting to love her job at Sunset Care Center and she felt so lucky to be getting payed just to spend time with such lovely lady's. She really enjoyed any time she spent with Julie and the golden girls; they were always a lot of fun. Ada still wasn't feeling well most of the time but her wonderful kids and grandkids were there about every day. The lady's in room 4, 5 and 6 used to spend a lot of time napping and watching TV. But now thanks to Erica's persistence they were playing cards in the lounge and even going to the yoga class. Most of the employee's at Sunset thought Trudy was a rich snob but Erica was really getting to know her and like her a lot. She got her to go eat at the cafe for lunch one day. Julie usually refers to her as Prude Trudy but she was super kind to her at the cafe that day and they made plans to sing a duet together one day soon. That was a big step for Trudy and Erica hoped that someday all the lady's in section C would be good friends.

Erica told Julie about Page saying her only son took his own life and Julie felt so bad for her that she started going to her room a couple times a week and playing a dice game with Page. Every once in a while when Julie's daughter Jesse came to visit, they would both go play dice with Page. That made Erica really happy.

It was a Friday afternoon, Julie was playing dice with Page, and the golden girls were over with the guys in their lounge playing monopoly. Ada was sleeping; the other lady's had visitors, so Erica went to spend some time with Trudy. Trudy looked so pretty. She had her hair done earlier that day and she was dressed in black pants and a very nice red

A

and black silk blouse. "You look so beautiful. Let me walk you over to the men's isle and you can hang out over there with the golden girls. They are all playing monopoly."

Trudy said, "I don't feel like it. I really want to talk to you anyway."

"What's up?"

Then Trudy said, "Remember when I told you that I had a secret that I wanted to tell you." Trudy got up and walked over and closed the door.

"Yes I remember you saying that."

"Well I want to tell you now. But it is confidential."

Erica curiously asked, 'What is it?"

Trudy pulled out a chair for Erica to sit down and then she sat down across the table with a very serious look on her face. "I need your help. And I am hoping your husband Nick will help too."

Erica couldn't imagine what she was going to say. "What can Nick and I do for you?"

"I have to tell you that I have not been a very nice person a lot of my life. I had a lot of money and it made me guarded. Whenever people tried to get close to me I always just assumed they were after my money and I would be ugly to them. I could be a down right bitch." Then she even got a tear in her eye and she said, "I can't even say it was only because of the money because I married into the money. When I was a child I was not rich and I wasn't a nice person then either. I was a bully and when I got

A

older in my teenage years I did some mean things, I don't know why. When I look back on my life I am not proud."

Erica started to interrupt but Trudy put her hand up like she always does when she doesn't want to be interrupted.

"There is a preacher that makes his rounds here at Sunset every Sunday." Trudy explained.

"Yes I met him. He is a really nice man."

She said, "Well I was talking to him one day and I told him I was afraid I wouldn't go to heaven because of the things I had done. He told me all I had to do is ask Jesus to forgive me and he would forgive me. He said that Jesus died so that we can be forgiven and all I have to do is ask. So I have asked for forgiveness and I am trying to be nicer. I do believe that Jesus forgives me but even though I am forgiven, I still regret treating people badly. I want to make up for it. I want to do something good so when I get to heaven I hear well done and not you can come in because you said sorry."

Erica asked, "So what is it you want to do and how can Nick and I help?"

Trudy said "Well this is the secret part, can I trust you?"

Erica couldn't imagine what Trudy was going to say, "Yes my lips are sealed you can trust me."

"Well I have some money put aside that my son doesn't know about. I would like for you to help me find some of the people that I hurt in the past so I can give them a gift. If you will help me I will give you a reward

A

too."

"That is not necessary; I will try to locate the people for you. Nick is very good on the computer. He can probably get you some addresses or phone numbers."

"Do you think your husband will help?"

"I don't know. I'm sure he won't mind searching the internet to try to find some people for you." Erica really didn't know what Nick would say.

"Well I want you guys to go and talk to the people in person, not on the phone. It's a lot to ask but you said you and Nick are bored and were looking for something to do, this could be like detective work and then when you find them I want you to bring them all to me so I can talk to them in person."

"How many people and do they all live in Missouri?" Erica asked as she walked over to the sink to get a drink of water.

"I don't have any idea where any of them are now but you said you can use a computer to find them, right. Tomorrow is Saturday. I would like you and Nick to come here together and I will give you the details." Trudy patted her hand on a manila envelope she had laying on the table.

Erica had so many thoughts going through her head. She wanted to do a good job at work and give the ladies all of her attention but to give up some of her weekend time too. Would Nick even be willing to consider it or would he think this was crazy. She told Trudy that she will ask Nick, but she didn't know if he will be willing. Then Trudy said with a big smile on

A

her face, "If you guys do this for me I will give you twenty thousand dollars."

"Twenty thousand dollars! Erica didn't know what to say, "I will ask Nick and if he agrees we will come see you tomorrow morning. Give me your cell phone number so I can call you in the morning and let you know either way."

Trudy wrote her phone number down on a piece of paper and handed it to Erica then pointed her finger at her and said, "This can give the two of you something to do together. I bet you will have more fun doing this than going bowling."

"I will call you in the morning." Erica winked at Trudy. As she walked out the door she was thinking how will looking for people and then going to tell them Trudy wants to talk to them be more fun than bowling.

A

Chapter seven

Erica couldn't wait to tell Nick what Miss Trudy asked them to do. She wasn't sure if he would say let's help the old lady or would he say is she senile? The first thing Nick said was, "Is she a crazy old lady? Erica I don't know if I believe she will give us twenty thousand dollars."

Erica said "I think we should go hear her out tomorrow. What if she really has that kind of money and gives it to us for helping? That would be awesome; it would really help our money problems. But it does sound too good to be true."

The next morning Erica bugged Nick till he finally agreed to go with her to meet Trudy.

When they walked into her room Trudy shouted, "Shut the door."

Nick shut the door and said, "Nice to meet you Trudy I have heard so much about you. I am Nick" he held out his hand to shake hers.

"Have a seat at the table." Trudy replied as she shook his hand.

Trudy puts a folder on the table and says, "This is all of the information I have on the people I want you to find."

She opened the folder. "The first one is a girl that used to work for me. Her name is Angie Sullivan. She worked at my 'Saving and Loan' in Florissant Mo about 24 years ago. I know that at the time she lived just right around the corner from work. I have the address of the saving and loan building but not her home address and I have no idea where she lives now or anything else about her except her mother was a maid at a hotel

A

that was right down the road from the savings and loan. I heard that Angie went to work with her mother after I fired her. But it was an old hotel so I doubt it is even still there or that she would still works there if it is. She is probably about 45 years old now. I want to find her and apologize to her because I fired her for absolutely no reason. I want to give her $20,000.00 but don't tell her that, just tell her I want to apologize and give her a gift."

"I also want you to find a boy named Tommy Davis. Well I guess he is not a boy now, he is a man but when I hurt him he was a boy. I know that is a common name so this might be hard and I really don't know anything else about him except his mom's name is 'Candy'. He is probably about 40 years old now."

"Is he someone who worked for you too?" Nick asked.

Trudy answered, "No, when he was just a little boy my husband Bob had an affair with his mother Candy. I found out about it and Bob and I split up for a while. But Bob begged me to forgive him and I finally did but before I took Bob back I went to Candy's house and knocked on the front door. Her husband answered and I asked if I could have a word with him, he let me in and I flat out told him that his wife slept with my husband. Just then his wife walked around the corner holding a little 3 or 4 year old boy in her arms. Her husband started confronting her about my allegations and she started to cry. The husband started screaming at her and I called her some very nasty names. I didn't feel bad at all about it at the time but when I think back about that night I remember that little boy crying so hard. I remember his mom put him down and he was standing

A

there looking up at his parents and crying hysterically as they screamed at each other. I heard later that Candy's husband left her. So I caused that little boy to grow up in a broken home. I want to say I am sorry and I want to give him $20,000.00."

Nick interrupted and said "Trudy, you didn't cause that little boy's pain. His mother and your husband did it. You should not feel bad about that."

Trudy replied, "I know I am not the one who did the sleeping around but I went out of my way to make sure Candy had to pay for what she did and I caused the little boy to hurt. I really want to tell him sorry."

Nick said "well then we will do our best to try to find him."

"Wait, there is one more, I mean two more. They are twins who grew up 2 doors down from me when I was a kid. Their names were Arleen and Darleen Cooper. They were a little bit younger than me so they are pretty old now, probably 75 or 76 years old. Everyone in school made fun of them because they had a speech problem. My mother told me to be nice to them, she said you need to be really nice to those twin girls and when anyone at school is mean to them you should stand up for them. But I didn't do it; I went along with all of the other kids. I actually think I was probably the one in school who made fun of them the most."

"So I know that my ugliness didn't come from having a lot of money because I was mean and ugly as a kid too."

Nick interrupted again, "Trudy all of us did stupid stuff when we were kids that we regret, I think you are being way too hard on yourself."

A

Then Trudy reaching for a Kleenex and blowing her nose said, "You don't understand Nick this is just three of the many mean things I have done. When I look back at my life there are just so many things I wish I would have done different. I am old now and I will spend my last few years here and my trust fund that my son has will pay for anything I need, so the money that I have hidden I don't need for anything. I want to do something good with it."

Nick asked," where is it hid? Is it in a bank?"

"No not in a bank. I don't want to tell you guys were it is just yet. I do trust you but it's a lot of money and if I tell you where it is you could get it and keep it all and I couldn't do anything about it. I really do trust you but sometimes that much money can cause people to do the wrong thing. Trust me I know."

"So you have over $80,000.00 that you have hidden somewhere?" Nick questioned.

Trudy shrugged her shoulders, "I really don't remember how much it is. When my son started talking to me about him being in charge of my money because he was worried about someone taking advantage of me, my main thought was I need to have some cash hidden so if I want things I won't have to ask my son. So I started taking out large sums of money out of the savings every couple of weeks and hiding it. I did this for about 3 months and that is when my son got a lawyer and declared me unfit to take care of myself. He thought that I was taking all of that money out and giving it away to charity's or something because when he would ask me what I was taking all of that cash out for I told him I spent it. I really am

A

not sure any more how much it is, but it is a lot. And they were going to have an auction to sell all of my stuff after I moved in here so I took some of my most expensive jewelry and put it in with the money. Oh and I also had a few rare coins that my husband Bob had bought years ago and I put them in with the money and jewelry."

"And you hid it all somewhere?" Erica scrunched up her face as she asked.

"Oh I put it all in a metal box and I hid it. I am not going to tell you where. I have been thinking about this for a long time and what I want to do is after you find the 4 people I told you about, I want you to bring them all to me and after I apologize, I will tell you where it is hidden and you can all go together to get it. That way there will be six of you getting the box for me and it will be more likely that you will bring it to me."

Then Trudy got a really worried look on her face. "Oh I hope I did the right thing trusting you guys. Please don't tell my son. He has more money than him and his kids could ever spend. I really want to decide what to do with my box of treasures. I know I could just give to charity but I can't stop thinking about all of the mean things that I have done and I want to tell some of the people I hurt that I am sorry. So I just feel like if I gave them something they would know that I am truly sorry."

Nick got up and gave Trudy a hug and said, "Our lips are sealed. We won't tell anyone and we will do our very best to find these people." and he picked up the folder and said, "Erica come on we got work to do."

As they walked to the door Trudy added, "All of the info I have on them

A

is in that folder. I hope you can locate them and if you do find them don't tell them about the money. Just tell them I want to apologize and that I want to give them a gift. After you find them all I would like for you to have them all come here on the same day. With them all here together I will apologize. Then I can tell you all where the money is and then you can go together to get it."

"Alright, we will keep you posted if we have any luck." Erica blew her a kiss as they walked out the door.

"Thank you both so much". Trudy blew a kiss back.

Nick winked at her and they left.

They didn't get out of the building without running into the golden girls who were on the way back from hanging with the guys. Betty said, "oh my goodness Miss Erica who is this hotty totty."

"Keep your hands off Betty he is mine," and as they walked out the door they could hear them all giggling.

A

Chapter eight

Neither of them said a word till they got in the car and then at the same time they both said "Oh my gosh!" Erica added, "This is just too good to be true."

"I think the old lady is a sweetheart and even if she doesn't really have all of that money I want to find these people for her." Nick started up the car and backed out.

While they were driving home they both started thinking of things they had done in the past and wondered if they needed to apologize to anyone.

Erica pouted, "When I was sixteen I ran over my best friend's kitten and I didn't tell her that I did it because I thought she would hate me forever."

"Erica that's terrible. Whose kitty was it, Ciara's?"

"No, it was Lindsey's, you don't know her. I haven't seen her in years."

"I've heard you talk about her before. Are you going to try and call her and tell her that you killed her poor little kitty?" Nick teased.

"I'm thinking about it." They pulled into the drive way, "I just want to concentrate on finding these people for Trudy right now."

"Me too let's get busy."

They went straight in the house and got on their computers and started to search. Nick was going to try to find something out about Tommy and Erica would search for Angie and they would search for the twins later.

Nick sat at the kitchen table with his lap top and Erica was lying on the couch with her I pad, both of them searched face book first with no luck. Nick found some really helpful web sites for searching for public records and a google blog search that was really helpful. Erica looked over the information that Trudy had in the folder about Angie. She worked at one of the loan companies that Trudy and her husband owned, it was on Florissant road and her mother worked at a hotel around the corner on Dunn road. Trudy wrote in her notes that she had heard that when she fired Angie she went to work at the hotel with her mother. It was about 25 years ago so the chances that she would still work at the hotel were slim but Erica started looking to find out what hotels were in that area. She wasn't as good with computers as Nick was so she asked him to help her and within a few minutes he gave her a phone number of a hotel on Dunn rd. right near Florissant road.

Erica called and asked if there was someone working their named Angie Sullivan. Her last name could be different if she had gotten married. The person who answered the phone said that there is a woman named Angie that works there. Erica asked if her last name was or used to be Sullivan. They did not know. So she asked how old about is she and the guy said "I don't feel comfortable giving you any more information. Now if you want to reserve a room, I will be happy to help you."

She hung up the phone and put her hands over her face and thought, "what if Angie had gotten married then her last name would be different.

A

How are we ever going to find her?"

Just then Nick said, "Bingo"

He had found an address for Angie Sullivan in Florissant Mo. "It is only an hour drive, let's go."

"Right now?" Erica tossed her I pad on the coffee table and picked up her coke.

"Its only noon, we can stop and get some lunch, and I will bring the I-pad and keep searching for Tommy if you will drive." He tossed her the keys.

Erica remembered that Trudy had said, it could spice up your boring marriage. You would be like detectives. So she guzzled down her coke and said, "Let's go detective Nick."

When they got up near St. Louis they stopped for lunch at a St. Louis bread company and had some soup and a sandwich. Over lunch Nick showed her that he had found 2 Tom Davis's and 2 T. Davis's living in and around St Louis. "No home address on this Tom but he is a manager of a McDonalds not too far from where his mother the adulteress Candy had lived." Nick said as he slurped his soup.

After they ate their lunch it was a short drive to the address they had for an Angie Sullivan. They both started to get a little nervous as they pulled into a trailer park and found the one with the number 22 on it. "This is it, 22 Oak Street." Nick said as he got out of the car and stretched his long legs. Erica's adrenalin was pumping as they knocked on the door. No body answered, so they got back in the car. "Should we ask some of the

A

neighbors about her?"

"I think we should try the hotel and see if she is the Angie that works there." Nick said as he got out the I-pad to get directions to the hotel. The hotel wasn't too far and they pulled in and went to the front desk.

The guy at the desk said that they have a maid named Angie and she is working right now. They asked him to call her up there so they could talk to her and he said she is working you will have to talk to her when she is off the clock. As they were walking back to their car they saw a cleaning lady pushing a cart around the corner of the building. They decided that Nick should stay in the car so that he doesn't scare her and Erica would go question the cleaning lady.

She went around the corner and found one of the rooms with the door opened. Erica peeked in and saw a woman taking the sheets off the bed. Erica knocked so she wouldn't startle her but she had head phones on and didn't hear her. Erica noticed that she looked to be in her 40's so maybe it was her. She had long black hair and was thin and very beautiful for her age but she had lines around her eyes that showed she wasn't a kid.

"Oh my God, you scared me! Can I help you?" the girl yelled and put her hand on her heart.

"Is your name Angie Sullivan?" Erica asked.

"Is it about my brother, is he in trouble?" then she put both hands on her heart. Erica tried to use a calm voice to calm her down. "No, I don't know your brother. A woman named Trudy Pelly is looking for you."

A

Trudy. I never expected what happened next."

Erica asked, "What happened?"

"The lady went psycho, that's what happened" Angie's voice got much louder. "She started calling me a gold digger. She yelled, I should have known that you would be after my money. If you think I am going to give you money to go to college you are out of your mind. Then she fired me and told me to get my stuff and get out."

Nick asked, "Did you tell her that you just wanted her help in picking what classes to take?"

"I didn't get a chance to. I was so shocked that she was talking to me like that, I was crying and I just grabbed my purse and left. I never went back there again. I ended up going to work with my mom at the hotel and I never did go to college."

"You could have still gone to college." Nick said.

"Even though I was going to get a grant for school, I still needed that job so I could afford transportation to and from college. I guess I just lost all faith in myself ever becoming anything after that. I really wanted to be just like Trudy. I thought I would make so much money and I would be able to get my sister some help with her drug problem and help my momma so she wouldn't have to work so hard. I would be someone for my little brother to look up to so he would want to stay away from drugs and maybe go to college too. Things could have been so different if that lady would have just helped me pick some damn classes to take and maybe give me some encouragement."

A

The waitress came to the table and set down a piece of cherry pie in front of Nick and a chicken sandwich in front of Angie. "Are you sure you don't want anything sweetheart?" she said looking at Erica.

"No thank you, I am still full from lunch."

Angie picked at her sandwich for a little while and then she started to cry. "My sister died about ten years ago from those damn drugs." She wiped her nose with her napkin. "My momma passed away last year and my brother has been in and out of jail and he is using drugs. Things would have been so different if I hadn't lost that job and if I would have went to college. The worst part is my mom having to bury her child. She never did get over it and my little brother was in jail when she passed away."

Nick said as he passed his pie over to Erica to have a bite, "Trudy must have realized that it was wrong to fire you and that is why she wants to apologize."

Angie took a couple of bites of her sandwich and then she said, "I sent her a letter about a week after she fired me telling her that I wasn't asking for money. I had a grant for college and all I was wanting was her advice because I had so much respect for her. Then I ended the letter saying that now I have absolutely zero respect for her and I hope I don't turn out to be anything like her."

She ate another bite of her sandwich and pushed the plate away and told them thank you for the food but please tell Trudy I don't want her gift or her apology. And then she got up from the table and started to leave. Erica tried to stop her but she was upset and said, "Please I just want to

A

go back to work now."

After she left Nick and Erica couldn't even finish the pie, "What should we do now? Do you think we should tell her that Trudy wants to give her a lot of money? Nick asked.

"Do you think she would even want the money or would she still say to tell Trudy I don't want it?" Erica exclaimed.

"Maybe she would want the money so she could help her brother. I know Trudy told us not to say anything about the money only to say she wanted to give a gift but if we don't tell her she will never go to see Trudy and it is obvious that she could use the money." Nick exclaimed.

Erica agreed that they should tell her it is a lot of money. They decided to give her some time to cool down and to come back when she gets off work. They decided to go get a hotel and stay the night but not at the hotel where she was working. It was a little run down. They found a nice place near the interstate. They would go try to talk to Angie again when she is off work and maybe go to that McDonalds in the morning and see if the manager named Tom was the guy they were looking for.

They relaxed on the hotel bed, both on the internet checking on other Tom's with the same last name in Missouri incase the McDonalds manager wasn't him.

"What time do you think she will get off work?" Erica poked Nick in the arm.

"I don't know, I think we should head over that way pretty soon and

A

watch for her to get off."

Erica said "we could just go to her house later on."

Nick said "we could but it might freak her out that we know where she lives. I think it would be better to wait for her at her work."

They drove back to the hotel Angie worked at and sat in the parking lot wondering what car was hers. They never did see her coming out of any of the rooms but it was a big place. Erica decided to go to the front desk and ask for her. The guy at the front desk started asking what do you want from her but then Angie came around the corner and saw her. Angie said, "I already gave you my answer."

"The guy at the desk said "is this lady bothering you?" "No, she nodded at him and said it was ok and then she walked outside with Erica.

"I just felt like I need to tell you one more thing." There was a bench out front of the hotel and the two of them sat down. Nick stayed in the car. "Trudy told me to only tell you that she wanted to give you a gift but I feel I need to tell you that the gift is a large amount of money."

"I didn't want her money then and I don't want it now."

"You said that if you had gone to college and made a lot of money you could have helped your sister and that it was Trudy's fault that it didn't happen. Well now maybe because of Trudy you can help your brother. You can use the money to help him."

"It's probably too late for my brother."

A

Erica convinced her that if she didn't take this opportunity, she will always wonder if she could have helped him if she had the money to get him help. Angie told her that she would think about it. She asked what nursing home Trudy was in just in case she did decide to go hear her apology. When Erica told her that the nursing home was about an hour away, Angie told her that she couldn't go anyway because she doesn't have a car. She told her that she walks to work or takes a cab when the weather is bad.

So Nick and Erica gave Angie a ride to her home and she invited them in. When they went in the house the kitchen window was open and some of Angie's stuff was missing. Angie was upset but she told them she knows that it was her brother. She told them that he was coming over all of the time asking for food or money. The last time she saw him she told him she wasn't going to give him anymore food or money so he started coming over when she was at work and he would just come in the window and take food.

"So I just stopped buying food so I would have nothing he could take. I have been eating at work or just buying enough for one meal and eating it. I know that sounds mean and it's not that I want him to be hungry. I was afraid I was being an enabler." Angie looked around her kitchen. All of the cabinets were open. "I think the only thing he took was a box of crackers that have been in the cabinet for a while."

She explained that he got out of jail about 6 months ago and he had got straight in jail but he is already back to using drugs and lately he has been acting really crazy. She figured he would be back in jail soon. Nick told her that is why she should let Trudy give her the money and it will be enough to get him in a good rehab. Before they left Angie agreed to go see Trudy. She gave them her cell phone number. They told her that they had three more people to find and after that they would come and pick her up and bring her to see Trudy.

A

Chapter nine

When they left Angie's house, Erica wanted to just go back to the hotel, but Nick told her it is only about a half hour drive to that McDonalds and he really wanted to go see if Tom was there. Erica was really tired but Nick thought that way if it's the wrong Tom when they get back to the hotel they can do some more searching. Then Sunday morning they would have all day to check out any other leads.

Erica stayed in the car and Nick went into the McDonalds and asked to talk to the manager. A young girl said "I'm the manager can I help you?"

When Nick told her he was looking for Tom she told him that he was not here but he would be working in the morning. So they headed back to the hotel and laid in bed searching the internet. Erica decided to start looking for leads on the twins while Nick did some more digging to find out which one of the Tom Davis's that live in Missouri had a mom named Candy.

By the time they went to sleep Nick found a lot more information on the other 3 Toms who lived in the area and he found out for sure that the McDonalds manager had a mother named Candy so he was most likely their man.

Erica found a death certificate for a Darleen Cooper and she found a retired school teacher named Arleen Cooper on Facebook. Her and Nick laughed as they looked at all of the stuff this lady named Arleen had put on Facebook she seemed like a hoot. They fell asleep around eleven pm.

A

The next morning they decided to pass on the complimentary breakfast, and go have breakfast at McDonalds. They ordered breakfast and sat down and started to eat. They saw a manager who looked to be about the right age to be him but he was really busy so they decided to eat first and hoped business would slow down so they could talk to him. A steady flow of people just kept coming in so Nick decided to just go up to the counter and ask to talk to the manager. He came over and asked if he could help him and Nick asked him to please come over and sit at the table so they could talk. He took off his apron and followed Nick over to the table.

Nick and Erica introduced themselves and asked him to sit down. They asked him if his mom's name was Candy. He said "Yes her name was Candy. She passed away a few years ago. What is this about?"

"Did your parents get divorced when you were about 4 years old?" Nick felt really awkward asking.

The manager started fidgeting in his seat with such a confused look on his face he answered "Well yes, I was 5 when they split up. Who are you guys and what is this about?"

Erica said "I'm just going to spit it out. I work at a retirement home and there is a woman that I take care of who claims that her husband had an affair with your mother and that is why your parents split up."

"Now hold on!" Tom interrupted. "If she wants money or something my mom is gone now and I am not responsible for anything she did in her past."

A

Erica reached over and grabbed his hand and said "It's the opposite; she wants to give you money."

The man looked even more confused. Erica explained to him everything that Trudy had told her about the day she came to his house and caused a big fight and that Trudy feels like she could have kept her mouth shut and maybe that little boy's parents would have stayed together. She told him that Trudy has a lot of money and she is old and she wants to apologize to him and to some of the other people she has hurt and she said she can't take her money with her so she wants to give it to some of the people she has wronged in the past.

Tom sat quiet for a minute. Then he told them he remembered that day. He was 5 years old. In fact it was his fifth birthday and his parents were going to take him to the zoo. His mom was telling him they were going to have so much fun and then a lady came to the door and his parents started yelling and the lady had a look of hate in her eyes and was cussing his mom out and they didn't go to the zoo and they did split up right after that.

He looked up at Erica and said, "That woman was hurt and that is why she came to our house that day. It certainly wasn't her fault that my parents split. It was partly her husbands fault and my mom's fault but even her husband wasn't to blame. My mother had other affairs besides that man so their marriage would have never worked out anyway. So you can tell her I accept her apology for ruining my fifth birthday because that is all she did. My mom was a piece of work, she made a mess of her life and it was nobody else's fault that her and my dad split up. So please tell your friend that I accept her apology for spoiling my birthday, but she surely doesn't owe me any money."

Erica said "The lady has plenty of money and if she wants to give some to you, you should take it."

"I wouldn't feel right doing that." Please just tell that women I accept her apology. Then he got up and went back to work.

"Should we be more persistent or should we just let it go?" Erica asked Nick.

"I guess we should just let it go. Do you have the address for that goofy Arleen lady?"

They got out their IPAD and started searching again. There was a web site that was very impressive on how much information they could get. Bingo! "Here is an address for her." It was in the opposite direction than home so Erica wanted to come back next weekend but Nick said we might as well check it out while we are here.

On the drive to her house Erica looked at more stuff on Arleen's face book page. Laughing she showed Nick a video of her singing a rap song. "This lady would get along good with Julie," Erica laughed.

They pulled up in front of a cute little house and got out and knocked on the door. They heard a voice yell, "Hold on I'm coming." A few minutes later she came to the door trying to open it holding a cane.

"Well hello are you Arleen?"

A

"Yes I'm Arleen, d-do I know you?" She stuttered. At that moment they knew they had the right person.

"Did you grow up on St Catherine Street and did you have a twin sister named Darleen?" Nick asked.

"Well yes I did." She said as she opened the door wider and motioned for them to come in.

"You two are way to-to yo- young to remember me f-from the old neighborhood."

"No we didn't grow up here but do you remember a neighbor or yours named Trudy?" at that moment they realized they didn't even know Trudy's maiden name.

"Well yes I remember Trudy. Sh- she was so pr- pretty. She lived ta- two doors up from me."

Erica explained to her that she worked at a retirement home where Trudy lives now and that Trudy feels bad because she was not very nice to her when they were kids. Trudy wants to apologize and give her a gift.

Arleen told them that a lot of people picked on her and her sister. She said that they were small for their age and they both had speech impediment so kids picked on them. That is just what kids do and there was no need for her to worry about it now. She told them it is water under the bridge. Then she offered them both a glass of sweet tea.

They both really liked the lady and they sat and talked to her for quite a while. They told her all about Trudy having some money hid and

A

her wanting to make things right with some of the people she had wronged. They told her about Tom and Angie. They made a deal that when they came up to get Angie to bring her to see Trudy that they would pick her up and bring her too.

"Even if you don't want to accept her gift you might as well go to see her and let her apologize to you. It might be fun to see someone from your childhood, "Erica tried to persuade her.

Arleen shook her head, "It would be great to s-see Trudy. S-s-since you all are offering to d-drive, I guess I may as well go."

They sat and visited and drank their sweet tea for about twenty minutes. Arleen gave them her phone number and they told her they would call as soon as they had a date picked out for the trip to see Trudy.

On the way home that afternoon the couple felt like very successful private detectives. Erica said, "I feel a little bit bad for telling all three of them about the money. Trudy asked us not to tell any of them and we told them all."

"If we didn't tell Angie she wouldn't have agreed to go see Trudy. Tom's not even going to go see her even after we told him about the money. Trudy really wants to do this so I think we did the right thing telling them about the money and at least two of the three are going to come and talk to Trudy."

Erica said, "I guess you are right. Should I call Trudy and tell her about our success?"

A

Nick thought for a minute, "I guess you might as well wait and tell her when you go to work tomorrow. That way you will be able to see the look on her face when you tell her."

The drive home seemed to go by really fast because they talked all the way home about their detective skills.

They both agreed it was a fun weekend but they were glad to be home and Erica couldn't wait to go to work the next morning and tell Trudy that they had found them all.

Chapter ten

When Erica got to work the next day she was rushing the lady's to get dressed and head down to breakfast because she couldn't wait to go talk to Trudy. Julie was up but not dressed and she said "I don't feel like getting dressed today." "Come on Julie you know the rules you have to be dressed to go to the café." "Well that's a dumb rule. I don't know why we can't all just stay in our jammys all day."

"I don't make the rules Miss Julie; I'll bring you a tray."

Ada wasn't feeling well again and she said she didn't want any breakfast so Erica thought she better be safe and take her down to see the nurse.

Miss Page was up and dressed and she headed down to the café without any problem but right before they got to the café Miss Page whispered, "We need to walk back to my room for a minute."

"What for?"

"I thought it was just gas but it wasn't."

So Erica walked her back to her room and waited while she cleaned herself up and then they walked back down to the café.

The golden girls were all in Betty's room putting on makeup. Erica tried to rush them but they all said, "You can't rush this! We want to look good today."

A

Erica told them. "Ok just don't be too long the serving staff is waiting."

After everyone was at the café Erica grabbed Trudy's tray and herself a muffin and headed to room ten.

Trudy was up and dressed and sitting at the table reading the paper when Erica walked in. "You won't believe it, we found them all." She put the tray on the table and pulled up a chair and sat down. "We went up to St. Louis on Saturday."

"You went up there, oh my goodness I thought it would take weeks of research before you would make a trip to find them. What happened, tell me everything."

"First of all we found Angie; she still works for that hotel. She remembered you and I guess, well I hate to tell you but she was still bitter after all of these years because she felt like her life would have been different if you hadn't fired her."

Trudy's face dropped, "did she say she would come here and let me apologize?"

Erica decided to spare Trudy the details about how Angie's sister and mother were dead now. That her brother was a mess and how Angie thinks it all is because Trudy fired her instead of helping her pick which classes to take. She didn't want to make Trudy feel sad. After all that was a long time ago and she was trying to do something nice now. "Yes she is going to come here. We told her we had a few more people to find and that after that we will call her and set up a time for everyone to come

A

here and let you apologize."

Trudy had a deep sad look on her face. "I can't believe she is still working at that hotel, I wish she would have gone on to college. She was a smart girl. It is really my fault, I broke her spirit."

Erica put her muffin down and went over and hugged Trudy. That was a long time ago and we can't change what happened but the important thing is that you are going to get an opportunity to apologize and give her a huge gift that I know won't make up for everything but it will really help her now. Come on eat your breakfast. The cooks really made some awesome pancakes and they are getting cold."

"Yes, you are right. I can't thank you and your husband enough for doing this for me." Trudy picked up her fork and took a bite of her pancakes. "Oh wow, these are really good."

Erica told her that her and Nick actually had a great time this weekend. She told Trudy that she was right it did spice up their marriage. It was like they were real private detectives. "We found Tommy; he is a manager of a McDonald's restaurant. He actually remembers the day very well it was his fifth birthday and they were going to go to the zoo. He remembers you coming to the door and his parents getting in a big fight. He said they split up right after that."

Trudy's face dropped again, "Oh my God, it was his birthday. I am a terrible person. No amount of money can change what I did. How will he ever be able to forgive me?"

"He said to tell you he forgives you for ruining his fifth birthday and

A

that is all you did. He said it was not your fault that his parents split. He said his mom fooled around with other men too. They would have split up weather you showed up at their house that day or not. He told me to tell you he understands why you came to his house that day. You were hurt and you don't need to apologize or give him anything."

Trudy pushed her plate away, "I can still see that little boys face when I was yelling at his mother. I want to tell him I'm sorry."

There was a knock on the door. It was the receptionist. She said, "Erica the nurse wants to talk to you about Ada."

"I'll be back later Trudy, eat your breakfast and stop being so hard on yourself."

The nurse said she was worried about Ada still not feeling well she couldn't find anything wrong but she wanted Erica to get ahold of Ada's family and tell them she wants her to go to the hospital for some test. Erica called Ada's daughter and told her that her mother was being sent to the hospital to get some test. She assured her that her mother was not any worse. She just is still not feeling her best and the nurse just wants to take precautions. Ada's daughter said she would call her siblings and to let her mother know that they will all meet her at the hospital.

It turned out to be a very busy morning; Julie was trying to climb up on a stool to put a new star on top of her tree and she slipped and scraped her shin. It was bleeding pretty badly when Erica came in to check on her. "For goodness sakes Julie how many times do we have to remind you that you are almost 90 years old? You cannot climb up on stools or jump on beds anymore. Come on let's go have the nurse take a look at it."

The nurse cleaned it up and bandaged it and she scolded Julie worse than Erica did. When they got back to Julies room Erica sang a song with her to cheer her up and then said do you want to eat lunch in your room or do you want to get some cloths on and go to the café. Julie said, "OH hell just bring me a tray, I aint getting dressed today."

Erica finally got everyone to the café for lunch, took a tray to Julie and went back and grabbed Trudy's tray and headed down to room ten. "Finally you are back, sit down I'm dying to hear about the twins. Did they remember me?" Trudy was so excited.

"I'm sorry Trudy, Darleen has already passed away, but Arleen remembers you."

"Does she hate me for the way I treated her and her sister?"

"Actually no, she doesn't hate you. She is doing fine; she lives in a cute little house by herself. When I told her that you would like to apologize for the way you treated her she said that there was no need. She said all of the kids made fun of her and Darleen, but that was a long time ago. It doesn't matter now but she did say she would love to come here and see you."

Trudy said "I can't thank you and Nick enough for doing this for me. It really means a lot. I still do want to apologize to Tommy and give him the money. Even though he says his parents would have gotten divorced even if I hadn't come over that day. I still can't get his little face out of my mind. Will you please ask him to come? Just tell him I have something for him."
A

Erica told Trudy she would get ahold of him and ask him to please come see her. She told her that if Tom agrees to come she will find out when is a good time for him and her and Nick would go get Angie and Arleen that same day so that they could all be here at the same time like she requested. Trudy was in such a good mood Erica talked her into going to Julie's room so they could sing that duet. She knew that would cheer Julie up and take her mind off of her leg.

Trudy's voice was a little shaky but actually she had a beautiful voice. She and Julie sang a couple of songs and then the golden girls came and joined them and then to everyone's surprise Miss Page decided to join them. It was a party in Julies karaoke lounge. Erica went down to the café and grabbed some snacks and soda's and brought them up to Julie's room. Erica could hear the Beatles music all the way down the hall. Everyone was having a lot of fun. They were singing the Beatles and Sony 'n' Cher songs and acting like a bunch of teenagers. It was like a scene from that movie cocoon. The party was still going on when Erica's replacement came and it was time for her to go.

 Cindy, the evening shift girl walked in and asked what in the world is going on and then she picked up a microphone and joined them. 'She's got a ticket to ride and she don't care. My baby don't care.' Was echoing through the hall way as Erica left for the night.

When Nick got home from work Erica was on the front porch drinking a beer. He got out of his car and said, "Who are you and what did you do with my wife? My wife never drinks beer!"

"It was a busy day at work and I needed something to calm me

A

down."

"Is everything ok?"

"Yes, everything is great. It was just a fast paced day all day." She said as she guzzled the last of her beer and then smashed the can with her hand, which made Nick laugh out loud. She told him about her day and they went inside and ordered pizza to be delivered. Nick got on line and found a phone number for the McDonalds that Tom works at. Then he called and asked to speak to the manager. "This is Tom can I help you."

Nick made a thumbs up to let Erica know it was him on the other line. "Hi Tom, this is Nick, my wife Erica and I were in there on Sunday and talked to you about the lady who wants to apologize to you."

"Oh hi Nick, yes I remember."

"We know that you said no apology was necessary but my wife talked to Trudy today and she really wants to do this. She said she cannot get your five year old face out of her mind. Is there any way you can come here and let her apologize? You would be helping an old lady have closure and peace."

"I don't know, let me think about it. It is kind of a long drive. Didn't you tell me you lived about an hour south of here?"

"Yes it would take you an hour or so to get here but remember she wants to give you some money. So that can make it worth your time and gas. We are only supposed to tell you that she wants to give you a gift but the gift is a good amount of money." Nick shrugged his shoulders and

A

winked at Erica.

"When do you want me to come?" Tom asked.

"How about this coming weekend? Actually we told the other two people who she wants to apologize to that we would come and get them because they don't have transportation. So we might as well get you while we are up there and then you won't even have to drive. What do you say?"

The doorbell rang and Erica payed the man for the pizza and took it into the kitchen and got out a couple of plates. Nick walked into the kitchen, "ok we will talk to you soon. Bye."

"He said he has a lot of vacation days saved up so he is going to see if he can get off this weekend and call me back."

Erica opened the fridge and got out 2 beers handed one to Nick and popped open the other one. "Let's celebrate!"

"I can't believe you are drinking 2 beers." Nick said as he grabbed a couple pieces of pizza and put them on his plate. CHEERS"

On Tuesday night Tom called Nick and said he can get this coming weekend off so he guesses he will come hear what the old lady wants to say. Nick told him he would call the other two people and make sure this weekend was good for them. Then Tom suggested that he just pick up the other two people and bring them down. He said he had an SUV with plenty of room and it would be silly for them to come all the way up there and get them all and drive back then have to do it again to bring them

A

back. Nick told him if he was sure he didn't mind that would be great. Erica called Angie and Arleen. Angie said she was off work on Saturday and Arleen said I'm free every day. So they text Tom the address and he said he would get an early start on Saturday morning and that he would call to let Nick and Erica know an exact time to meet them all at Sunset Care Center.

Trudy was so happy to hear the news. She couldn't believe how fast Erica got this all to work out. She told Erica that her and Nick were damn good detectives.

Ada's test finally came back on Friday and it was bad news. She had cancer. She was going to have to go back to the doctor at the hospital on Monday to discuss her options. All of her kids were there with her and Ada was keeping a good attitude.

Chapter eleven

Nicks phone rang at about ten am Saturday morning. It was Tom, he said, "I have Angie and Arleen in my car and we are headed that way. We should be there at about eleven."

"Great we will see you in a little while."

Nick told him that they would meet them all at the front door at the Care Center and that he would have his phone handy if they had any trouble finding it to call. So Erica and Nick got to Sunset at around 10:30 to make sure Trudy was dressed and ready. When they got to her room she was all ready for them. So Erica and Nick went out front and sat on a bench to wait. A red SUV pulled in the parking lot at exactly eleven. "I bet that's them." Nick and Erica said at the same time.

They saw Angie get out of the front passenger side and open the back door, so they walked over to greet them. As Arleen struggled to get out of the car with her cane, she said "These two flirted with each other all the way here."

Angie butted in, "You are the one who was flirting. You didn't sit back in your seat the whole time. You kept on touching Tom's shoulder and giggling like a little school girl."

"Girls, stop fighting over me. There is enough of me to go around." Tom laughed.

Everyone laughed and they headed toward the building. When they all walked into Trudy's room she got up and thanked everyone for coming

A

and gave everyone a hug. She was crying. Erica had seen her tear up a time or two but she had never seen her cry like this before. Everyone took a seat at her table. Erica had to go next door to Clair's room and borrow two more chairs. She was glad that Clair wasn't in her room so she didn't have to take the time to explain what was going on. She brought in the chairs and her and Nick sat down.

"I'll start with you Tom. They tell me you said that I didn't owe you an apology because I just came to your house that day because I was hurt." Tom nodded. "Well, yes I was hurt that my husband did what he did but I went to your parents' house that day because I was going to get that woman back. I know I had so much hate in my heart and I went there hoping to get her back and cause her pain. I saw the pain I caused you that day and I didn't care. You were just a little innocent boy and when I look back on the whole thing I wish I would have handled everything differently. I can't tell you how much it means to me that you forgive me."

Tom got up and gave Trudy a hug and said, "I do forgive you. It's been long forgotten by me. Now you need to forget it."

Then Trudy looked over at Arleen. "How can you ever forgive me, I was so cruel?"

"A lot of kid's pi-pi-picked on me and my s-s-sister. I got used to it a long ti-time ago. I think you are being w-w-way too hard on yourself."

Just then Angie busted out crying and all eyes turned to her. Erica grabbed Angie's hand.

"I guess I'm the only one who doesn't think you are being too hard

A

on yourself. I worshiped you. I wanted to be just like you. You hurt me so much. My life could have been so much different if you weren't so mean."

Angie and Trudy were both crying so hard. Erica grabbed a box of Kleenex and put them on the table and tried to stay strong and not cry herself.

Finally after about 5 Kleenex Trudy spoke in a soft voice. I got your letter after I fired you and I realized that I had judged you wrong. I have no excuse. I read your letter and you even sent the paper showing that you had received a grant and you truly didn't need my money. But I was too proud to pick up the phone and apologize. That is what was wrong with me. I was always too proud and I always thought everyone that tried to get close to me just wanted my money. I wish I could go back in time and do everything different. If I could start over I would be so generous and I would have traded my cold stone heart for a soft loving heart."

Nick smiled at Trudy and said, "Miss Trudy that is what you are doing now. It takes a lot for someone who is proud to apologize. I think you did trade your heart in because I am seeing someone with a soft and loving heart."

Angie had rehearsed all week about how she was going to tell Trudy that she once had so much respect for her and that now she had absolutely no respect for her and that it was her fault that her sister was dead and her poor momma had to suffer. She planned to say I will not accept you apology not now or ever. But now after hearing her heartfelt apology, Angie had a whole new respect for her.

A

Just then Trudy's, Saturday delivery from her favorite restaurant arrived. She had called ahead and asked them to bring enough for six. So they all sat around the table and enjoyed a delicious meal. After everyone had ate all that they wanted Trudy spoke up and said, "I want to give all of you a gift."

Then she told them all about how right after her husband died her son started talking to her about putting him in charge of her estate. She knew it was only a matter of time before he would talk her into doing it so she started taking cash out of the bank and putting it in a shoe box in her closet. She did this once a week for over a year. Then when her son hired an attorney to get the process started she started taking large sums of money out and putting it in the shoe box. She told them that she had a shoe box full of one hundred dollar bills and more money that she couldn't even fit into the box. Then she ordered a metal fire proof box on line and put the shoe box, some loose cash and some of her jewelry and some rare coins in the box and buried it in her back yard.

They all sat there not believing what they were hearing. Trudy laughed and said, "The box was pretty heavy, I had to put it in a wheeled barrel and wheel it out to the back of my yard and it took me all day to dig the damn hole." There were a few giggles around the table everyone picturing this old woman digging a hole.

She told them that she had a pet cemetery in the back of her yard where they had buried their family pet's years ago. There was a dog named Buddy and two cats Charlie and Frank. Each one had a rock head stone with their names painted on it. Every couple of years Trudy would

A

touch up the paint on the stones and re mulch the area. She told them that she went in the woods behind her house and found a flat stone and painted the name Goldie on it. She spread some mulch around the new grave and put the wheeled barrel away and got cleaned up just in time because later that night her son showed up with his attorney.

"I was so afraid that they were there because someone saw me bury the box. My heart was pounding. They came in and started questioning me about the large amounts of cash I had been taking out. When I couldn't think of anything to say that I had spent it on, my son accused me of being too forgetful. I guess I was just so happy that they weren't there to ask me what I just buried in my back yard. Then before I knew it I was signing a paper for my son to be in charge of my estate."

Nick asked, "Are you wanting us to go dig up the box?"

"I figured you could go in the middle of the night or at least late at night while everyone is asleep. There is a strip of woods behind the house. You could park on the street behind the woods and go through the woods right into my old backyard. I have already made a map of the area and a map of my yard. She opened up a folder and pointed to an x on a piece of paper. Right here is Goldie's grave." She looked up and winked. "I want you all to go together so that nobody is tempted to take the whole box and run."

Angie spoke up, "What if the people who bought your house didn't want your pets buried in their yard and moved them or maybe just moved the stones?"

A

Trudy said, "Well when my house sold, before I moved out. I called the realtor and told her that I had a small pet cemetery in my yard and because I was moving into a nursing home I would like to leave them right where they are. I would like to know if the buyer's had a problem with it because if they did I would find somewhere to move them. She called me right back and she said that the buyers saw the little cemetery when they looked at the house and they do not mind if you leave it there. They have pets and will someday add to it. So unless they were lying it should still be there."

"When are we supposed to do this?" Tom asked.

"How about doing it tonight?" Trudy screeched clapping her hands together. "I don't want you guys to pry open the box or anything. I want you to bring it to me and we will all open it together. I have the key right her." And she pulled a chain with a key on it out of her pocket.

Erica looked around the table at everyone else and said, "It is a long drive up there and back but Nick and I are free tonight and off work in the morning."

Tom said that he took the whole weekend off so he was in. Arleen said she didn't have any plans, but Angie said Saturday was her only day off and that she had to be to work early in the morning.

"Trudy said, "Your calling in sick tomorrow honey!"

"I guess I could, I haven't missed a day in over a year. I don't get paid if I don't show up though." Angie thought to herself out loud.

A

"If you guys pull this off and bring me the box here in the morning, I will give you a lot more money than you would have made working"

They all leaned over the maps and ask Trudy all of the questions that they could think to ask. They decided that if they all could fit comfortably in Toms SUV they would all ride together. Tom thought maybe they should leave Arleen there with Trudy and the rest of them go. But Trudy wanted her to be there at least waiting in the car. She said, "With 5 of you the odds are better that you won't take the money and run."

Erica leaned over and kissed Trudy on the cheek, "I promise we won't take your money and run. I love my job here so much I am not going anywhere. We will be back but we will probably stay the night in St Louis and come back down here in the morning."

"Then I want you all to spend the night together in the same hotel room so that nobody is alone with the money."

Tom said, "Everyone can stay at my house, I have enough room and I don't live too far from your old house."

A

Chapter twelve

The ride up to St Louis was a lot of fun and went by fast. Nick sat in front with Tom and the three girls sat in the back. Arleen kept joking about how she is old and she should have got to sit in front with Tom and then she would reach up and rub his back. Then she would look at Angie and say he is mine. Then Tom would say girls, quit fighting over me. They joked around all the way. It was only about 4:00 when they got there so they drove through Trudy's old neighborhood to scope it out. Her house was absolutely gorgeous. They found a place on the street behind her house to park and made all of the details for their grave robbery for later that night. Then they decided to go to Tom's house to hang out until it was time to go rob a grave.

They ordered pizza and played Nintendo. Angie called her boss and told him she couldn't make it in to work the next day.

Erica whispered to Nick, "I think Angie and Tom like each other."

"Da, it is obvious that they do and Arleen is jealous." He laughed.

At 11:00 pm they decided to head on over to Trudy's old house. Arleen was asleep on the couch. Erica started to wake her up and Angie said, "can't we just leave her here?"

Arleen's head popped up, "don't you dare leave me here." She hobbled toward the bathroom and patted Tom with her cane as she walked by. "I know Tom wouldn't go without me."

A

By the time they finally got Arleen in the car it was 11:20, and it was about a 25 minute drive to Trudy's old neighborhood. It was a beautiful July evening, with a slight breeze. The moon was about ¾ full so it was bright enough outside that they decided that they wouldn't need a flash light. They arrived a little bit before midnight. The plan was for Arleen to wait in the car. The other four would walk through the woods; the two men would find the grave marked Goldie and start digging. They brought a shovel and a pick. Erica and Angie would watch the house and they were supposed to caw like a crow if they saw anyone. If anyone hears a caw sound they should start running through the woods back to the car.

"I'm so nervous how about you?" Erica whispered to Angie as they walked through the wood.

"Shh" both guys replied.

"I hope I don't step on a snake!"

"SHHHH!!!"

The guys found the little grave yard area right where Trudy's little map showed it would be and they located the one marked Goldie. The girls walked just a little toward the house and stood behind a tree. The house was completely dark but all at of the sudden a back porch light came on.

"CAW CAW"

They all made a mad dash through the woods. Erica tripped on a log and scraped up her shin, but her adrenaline was pumping. She got right

A

up and ran to the car. The two girls yelled move over to Arleen and jumped in the back seat. Nick practically threw the shovel and pick into the back seat with the girls and he jumped in the passenger's side front seat and Tom took off.

"Ouch Nick you hit me with that pick right where I am already bleeding from falling."

"I'm sorry honey; I didn't want to take the time to open the back hatch. What happened did someone come out side? Do you think they saw us?" He sounded a little more worried if someone had been seen than he was about his wife's leg right now.

Erica said, "I didn't see anyone but the back porch light came on."

"Oh my God, what if it's just a motion light and a tree limb or something triggered it to come on?"

Angie said, "I think I heard a screen door open did you hear that Erica?"

"No I just saw the light and started running and cawing."

Tom pulled into a convenience store parking lot so they could park and talk about what to do now. Nick questioned Angie about the screen door she thought she heard. She couldn't be sure either way. They decided to drive by the house and see if any lights were on.

Tom pulled out of the parking lot and around the corner and headed back to Trudy's old house. The house was completely dark so they drove around the corner and back around to the store to park and talk about it

A

again.

Nick said I bet it was just a motion light and he thought that they should go back and finish the job. Tom thought they should go home and sleep for a while but set the alarm for about 3:00 in the morning and come back. Erica agreed with Tom.

But then Angie came up with a great idea. "I have an idea you guys. We can go to my place and get my maid's uniform. Then in the morning I could knock on their front door and I say I used to be a cleaning lady for Trudy who used to live here. Then I will say that she let me burry my dog in her back yard because I lived in an apartment and had nowhere else to bury him. Now I just got married and this is my husband." She pointed to Tom. We just bought our own house and I was wondering if you would mind if I got my dogs remains and moved him to my new home."

"It's brilliant!" Erica clapped her hands, "How did you just come up with that?"

Nick said, "I think it's too risky, because if they don't let her do it then they will be suspicious and dig it up their selves." Tom agreed with Nick.

"If we go back tonight that is risky because if they did see us earlier they will be watching for us and we will get caught."

"The whole house was dark when we just drove by, I am sure they went back to bed." Nick argued.

"It would make sense to keep the lights off and watch for us." Erica pointed out.

A

"With a house that expensive they would have called the police if they saw us."

They went back and forth not being able to decide what to do. So they decided to take a vote. Tom and Nick both agreed that they thought going back at three am was the best idea and Angie and Erica liked the maid idea. "Well you are the deciding vote Arleen, Arleen." She was sleeping, sitting strait up with her eyes closed and sound asleep. Angie slapped her leg, "No wonder she has been so quiet."

"What's going on? Are we g-going back to r-rob the grave now?"

"No we are voting on what to do. You will be the deciding vote," They told her the guys want to go back at three in the morning and try again. Then they told her Angie's idea.

"I l-l-like Angie's idea. All accept the-the part where T-tom is her husband." Arleen giggled.

"Come on be serious."

"I am s-serious, he is my man." Arleen winked at Tom.

Erica said, "Ok Nick will play her husband now how do you vote?"

"I think the m-maid idea is the b-b-best idea also I d-don't want to get up at 3 am."

Tom starts up the car and pulls out of the convenience store lot, "I guess either way, we might as well go home and get some rest right now. The two guys were talking like they were still planning to go back later in the night. Arleen got a wet wipe out of her purse and cleaned up Erica's leg. Angie tapped Tom on the shoulder and said, "The girls won the vote you need to get off at the next exit to go by my house so I can get my uniform." Tom looked over at Nick and he shrugged his shoulders. Tom got off at the next exit and Angie directed him to her mobile home.

They pulled up to her place and she said, "It will just take a second, be right back."

When Angie was out of sight Arleen said, "Boy her p-p-place is sm-smaller than mine."

It was about 5 minutes before Angie finally came back out to the car. They were just about to go check and see if everything was all right. She looked like she had been crying when she got back in the car.

"What's w-wrong with you?" Arleen blurted out.

Everyone looked at Angie as she wiped her eyes with her uniform. "Nothing, just my brother must have broken into my house again. I guess he was looking for cash. All my drawers were pulled all the way out and stuff was turned over. He made a big mess."

"We need to call the police." Tom demanded.

"NO! I will not call the police on my brother. He gets in enough trouble from them without my help. Let's just go back to your house Tom."

"How can you be sure it was him and not a thief?" Tom questioned with a concerned look on his face.

A

"I'm sure, please let's just go." They drove all the way to Tom's house not saying a word. When they got there they had to wake Arleen up again. Tom showed Arleen to his guest bed room. He offered for her take a shower if she wanted but she just got right in bed and told him that she was too tired. Then she said, "Good night cutie-pie."

They all decided that they would do Angie's plan and go in the morning and knock on the door. Angie told them she was a good actress and she can pull it off. They thought it would be best if just 2 of them went to the door and the rest wait in the car. They also decided they better go early because it would be Sunday and the people who live there might go to church. Tom got an air mattress and pump out of his hall closet and plugged it in to blow it up. He insisted that Nick and Erica take his bed and Angie the air mattress and he would sleep on the couch.

After Nick and Erica finally gave in and went to bed in Tom's room, Angie crawled under the sheets on the air mattress and Tom got himself a pillow and blanket and lay on the couch. Angie and Tom talked for a while about her brother. Then Tom set an alarm and they all went to sleep.

The alarm started blaring at 6:00 am. Tom got up and started a pot of coffee. Angie pulled the sheet over her head and went back to sleep. At about 6:30 Tom started waking everyone up. Nick and Erica got right up. Tom brought Angie a cup of coffee and pulled the sheet off of her face and said, "How do you like your coffee Julia Roberts."

"What, my name isn't Julia."

"You're an actress this morning remember."

"Black is fine." She sat up and took the cup from his hand and started sipping.

"Now to try and wake up Arleen." Tom started down the hall way with another cup of black coffee.

"Good luck."

He came back down the hall, "She's awake but she likes cream and sugar."

After they all had a cup or two of coffee they all squeezed back into Toms car and headed to McDonalds. Tom called ahead for them to have food ready for them all. When they walked in the front door a young girl behind the counter said Good morning Tom, I put your order on table 8. He guided them all around the corner and they all sat down.

On the table were 5 trays. Each one was loaded with coffee, orange juice breakfast sandwiches, hotcakes and hash browns. As they sat down Arleen said, "My m-man has s-some clout."

They all pigged out and talked for a while about the plan. They just hoped that the people would be home. "If they aren't home I think the yard is private enough to sneak back through the woods and just dig it up fast and get out of there." Nick tried to convince.

"I think that is just too risky. They might have surveillance cameras." Erica worried.

"I never thought about that, let's just hope they are home and that they buy Angie's story."

A

They got to the house later than they had hoped. It was almost 9:00. Angie and Nick walked up to the door. The rest of them stayed in the car parked in the street in front of the house. Arleen was asleep sitting up again in the back seat.

Angie was dressed in her maid uniform and Nick was in jeans. They knocked on the front door. Angie's heart was beating so hard Nick could hear it. A young man dressed in very nice clothes, who only looked to be about 30 years old, answered the door. "Are you the man of the house?" Angie said nervously.

"Yes I am, can I help you?"

Angie felt a little less nervous with him being so young. "My name is Angie; I use to be a cleaning lady for Miss Trudy, who used to live here. I worked for Trudy for 5 years. This is going to sound crazy but back when I worked for her I had a dog named Goldie and Goldie died. I lived in an apartment and didn't have anywhere to bury my dog so Miss Trudy let me bury her in her back yard. This is my husband Nick. We just got married and we bought a house and I would like to move Goldie to my own back yard. Would you mind if we went in your back yard and get my dogs remains? We will fill the whole in and clean up the area."

The man looked in deep thought and then he said, "Did you come here last night sneaking around in my back yard trying to dig up your dog?"

Angie's heart started beating loud again. She didn't know what to say. She hadn't rehearsed this. "I'm sorry yes we did."

A

The young man laughed. "I fell asleep on my couch last night and woke up about midnight and I went out my back door to have a smoke and I heard what sounded like a girl saying caw caw and then I thought I heard people running through the woods. Then I heard a car start up and drive away. I got out a flash light but I didn't see anything missing so I went to bed." He smiled and shook his head. "I guess it was you two."

"I am so sorry it was not right of us to come on your property without your permission." Nick spoke up.

The man said, "I told my wife about it this morning and she was mad at me for not calling the cops."

Just then his wife came to the door. She was a beautiful young blond with blue eyes, dressed in a little pink skirt outfit. She looked like a teenager. Her husband told her, "These are the people who I heard in our yard last night." Then he explained to her what was going on.

The young women shook her head and said, "I don't think it is right to move that grave. You can go back there now and pay a visit to your dog but I don't want you digging her up."

Angie had tears in her eyes and she said, "Oh please mam, it would mean so much to me to have her in my own back yard. She is the only pet I have ever had and I loved her so much." Nick was amazed at what a good actress Angie was.

Back in the car Tom and Erica were starting to get worried, "It doesn't look like it is going well." Tom said staring out the window.

A

"I know I'm nervous." Erica said biting her nails.

Angie's tears started running down her face, "Oh please mam." She sobbed.

"I'm afraid that after this much time your dog is going to be decomposing and the bones will just fall apart into the dirt. It's just not a good idea." The young lady said as she gave Angie a hug.

"She is in a metal box. Miss Trudy gave me a very nice metal box to bury her in."

"Oh OK then I guess it would be alright. You really loved that dog didn't you hun?"

"Yes I did." Angie sobbed. "Thank you so much, this means a lot to me."

Nick headed to the car to tell the others what was going on and to get the shovel. "Who are those people in the car?" the girl asked Angie.

"They are just some of my friends." Angie answered.

"They don't have to stay in the car, they must be hot."

"They will be fine. We will just get this done and leave you alone. I am so sorry to be bothering you on your weekend." Angie just wanted to get the box and get out of there.

The man said, "We do need to be leaving for church in a little while and I do want you off our property before we leave."

A

Nick returned with the shovel and they all walked around the house on a cobble stone sidewalk which winded through a beautiful flower garden. The back porch and yard was amazing. It was a beautiful summer day and the smell of flowers filled the air. Angie had never seen a more beautiful yard in her life. They walked back to the back corner of the yard where the pet cemetery was. The mulch on the grave marked Goldie was all pushed to the side.

"The man said "I guess that is all you got done last night was move a little mulch when I came out for a smoke, you must have just started to dig."

"Ya, I had just moved the mulch when Angie yelled caw. Again we are so sorry." Nick answered and started to dig. The young couple stood there watching.

Angie started with the fake tears again and asked if they would mind giving them some privacy. The man folded his arms but the young girl said come on honey this is a sacred moment for her and she grabbed his arm and they walked up to the porch and sat on their swing.

The box was only buried down about a foot. Trudy probably couldn't dig any deeper so she had just put a mound of top soil and mulch on top of the grave. When Nick pulled out the box he thought they are going to know this isn't a dog. The medal box was about 3' by 2' but only about 1" deep. It was just a funny shape for a dog casket, maybe if it was a small dog but it was awful heavy to be a small dog.

Angie whispered to Nick that she had almost said her dog was a golden retriever. "OH thank God you didn't."

Angie took off her maid's apron and put it over the box. "Why don't you go around the other side of the house so you don't have to walk right past them and I will go over and tell them thank you."

"Good idea, but first I need to fill in the hole." He set the box covered with the apron down and Angie leaned over it like if she was praying. After nick filled in the hole and spread the mulch out to make the spot look nice he picked up the box and headed around the other side of the house and out to the car. Angie picked up the shovel and the rock that had Goldie painted on it and walked up to the back porch. The young couple was still on the swing. Angie had dirt smeared tears on her face.

"Do you mind if I take Goldie's head stone."

"Of course not Honey. Just get that box home and buried." And she gave Angie another hug.

"That's why I have my friends in the car. We are going to have a funeral when we get back to my place." Angie replied as she carried a shovel and a rock around the house on the cobble stone walk. The couple walked her around the house and waved bye to Nick as he was getting in the car. Angie heard the man say as she was walking to the car. "Strange girl!" Then she heard the women say, "She must have really loved that dog."

Everyone breathed a sigh of relief as they drove away. "I can't believe we did it." Erica exclaimed.

A

Nick said, "It was all Angie's idea and she was an amazing actress. She even had fake tears. How did you do that Angie?"

"Every time I think about my mom at my sister's funeral, I can't help but cry. So I just forced myself to think about that and the tears just came." Then she started to cry again.

"Trudy was cr-crazy to fire you g-girl!" Arleen put her arm around Angie and everyone else in the car agreed with Arleen.

"I called Trudy and told her what was going on while you guys were in the back yard digging up the grave. I guess I should call her back and tell her that you were successful." Erica started to dial the phone.

"Don't call her." Nick looked in the back seat and knocked Erica's phone out of her hand. "Let's leave her in suspense."

"I th-think we should p-p-pull over and pry that box open. If it's as m-much m-money as Trudy said it was w-we should all go to the B-B-Bahama's." Arleen chuckled and reached up and squeezed Tom's shoulder.

Erica slapped Arleen's leg, "We are bringing the box strait to Trudy."

Chapter thirteen

The drive back seemed like it took forever. They finally pulled into the parking lot at Sunset Care Center. Erica told Tom to drop her off at the front door and for him to pull around and park in back. She said "I will get the key and let you all in the back door. If the golden girls see us all walking down the hall with that box they will start asking questions and they won't leave us alone."

"Good idea." Tom dropped her off and they pulled around back.

Erica went in and went to the office to get a key to the back door. "Hey girl, what are you doing here on a Sunday?" Jazmin, one of Sunset's receptionists asked.

"I just have something I need to talk to Trudy about." Erica said as she grabbed the key.

"Girl you love these lady's, don't you? They lucky to have you, girl." Jazz said as Erica smiled and walked out of the office. She headed over to section C. Everyone was in the café finishing up lunch so she didn't have to talk to anyone else. Trudy's room was at the end of the hall and the back door was right there.

Erica was opening the door when Trudy came rushing out of her room. "Did you get it?"

"See for yourself." Erica pointed out the door to the rest of the group walking across the back parking lot with a medal box covered in dirt.

Trudy looked like a little kid at Christmas, clapping her hands in

A

excitement. They all went into her room and put the box on her table. Trudy pulled the chain with the key on it out of her pocket. She sat quit for a second and looked around at everyone. "Thank you all for forgiving me and for doing this for me. Someone please shut the door and lock it." Nick went over and locked the door. Everyone was so excited while Trudy fidgeted with the key opening the box.

She opened the box and there were hundred dollar bills everywhere. Trudy pulled the loose money out and was stacking it with her hands but there were so many bills she couldn't hold them all in her hand. She asked Erica to get her the bag of rubber bands out of her top desk drawer. Trudy counted out fifty bills and handed them to Erica to rubber band together then she did it again and again and again. "Oh my god, this is twenty thousand dollars." Erica said holding the four stacks of five thousand each.

"That is for you and Nick."

"We can't take this much money from you Trudy." Erica said handing the money over to Trudy.

"It's yours, you did what I asked you to do and I am a woman of my word. I want you to have it."

Trudy pushed the money over in front of Erica. Then she reached in the box and pulled out a plastic bag with some coins in it. It was only a few coins but she said they are very rare. She opened the bag and pulled one out took her glasses from around her neck and put them on. "This is an 1856 flying eagle. I believe it is worth about $20,000 and she set it on the table and pulled out another coin. This is a 1904 Morgan, I think it is

A

worth about $13,000 and the last one is a 1836 reed edge half. It is worth about $13,000 also."

"Wow, where did you get these?" Tom asked as he picked them up and examined them.

Trudy told them that her husband had a good friend who would borrow money for his house and cars and even for his business from our loan company. "He got into some trouble and lost his business. He owed us quite a bit of money but we didn't want to foreclose on our friend. He gave us the coins and told us what they were worth. They were only worth about one fourth of what he owed us but he was a good friend so we took the coins. He said he will pay us the money he owes us when he gets back on his feet, and we can give the coins back when he does. Well he never did pay us back, so I still have the coins."

They passed around the coins. Then she pulled out a couple of boxes that looked like they contained jewelry. She opened one of the boxes and it was ear rings. These are red diamonds. Then she opened the other box and it was a matching necklace. My husband bought these for me for our 25 anniversary. I had a lot of jewelry but this was always my favorite. My son sold most of my stuff in an auction when I moved here but I put these in my box. I remember my son asking me about them and I just played dumb. They are a one of kind and they use to belong to an actress. What's her name? I can't think of her name right now but he bought them at a celebrity auction for charity." Everyone passed around the jewelry and Angie asked if she minded if she put on the necklace. "Of course not, put it on. It will make you feel beautiful."

A

"C-c-can I put it on next?"

"Just a minute, let me wear it for a minute." Angie slapped Arleen's hand.

Then Trudy pulled out the shoe box. It was a pretty big shoe box and when she took the lid off everyone gasped. It was full of one hundred dollar bills. They were rubber band together in bundles of $5000. The box was stuffed full. She reached in and took out 4 bundles and handed them to Tom. "I want you to have this."

Before Tom could say anything she held up her hand like she always does and said, "I don't want to hear anything you are taking it."

Then she pulled out four more bundles and she said, "Arleen, This money does not make up for me treating you the way I did. When I think back I remember you and your sister always friendly, always kind you didn't do anything to deserve for me or anyone else to pick on you. It's not that I am trying to buy your forgiveness, I just will feel better if you take it so please except it for me."

"I guess I w-will take it if y-y-you insist." Arleen giggled.

Then Trudy looked over at Angie, both of them teared up. "A lot of people tried to get close to me because of my money and when you asked for my help, I just assumed that you wanted money." Then she bust out crying.

Angie tried to say something but she put up her hand like she always does. "Here I am trying to make excuses. I don't have an excuse. I was

A

wrong, I was a total bitch. Especially because when I got your letter explaining that you only wanted help picking classes. You even sent proof that you had a grant. I remember saying to myself. Sure, and I threw the letter away and never talked to you again. Angie, the fact that you are sitting here shows that you are a bigger person than me. You are a much bigger person than me. Please except this." And she handed her 4 bundles.

Angie sniffled and said, "I never gave any thought about how it was to walk in your shoes, Trudy. I don't know what it would be like to be rich and never know if people really liked you or if they just wanted something from you. I am sorry for not being more understanding of you."

Everyone was quiet for a minute or so. Then Tom broke the silence, "How much money is in that shoe box anyway."

"I don't even know and I'm not going to count it." She closed the shoe box lid and put it back in the medal box. Then she placed the plastic bag with the three coins and the small box of ear rings into the medal box. "That is how much I trust you Erica; I want you to keep this medal box at your house for me because this is just too much money for me to have in this room."

"What are you going to do with the rest of it?" Erica asked.

There was a knock on the door, "Can I come in Miss Trudy? Have you finished your lunch?" it was Carla the weekend aide.

"I have company can you come back later?"

A

"Sure I'll come back late, dear."

Trudy started to talk and there was another knock on the door. "I said I have company, what do you want?"

"It's me, Betty. Do you want to sing karaoke with us?"

"I have company right now."

"You have K-k-karaoke here. Can I go s-sing?"

"Hold on Betty, there is someone here who wants to sing." Erica yelled toward the door. "Ever since I met you Arleen, I have been thinking that you would get along good with most of these lady's. Let me introduce you to them." Erica helped Arleen up and they opened the door. She introduced Arleen to Betty and then she walked down the hall with them and introduced Arleen to Julie and the other two golden girls. Arleen must have been a little bit nerves because she started stuttering really bad. Erica wondered how she was going to sing karaoke.

Julie said, "You are company so you pick the first song," and she handed Arleen her binder with all of her songs listed in alphabetical order. Erica knew that Arleen was in good hands with Julie so she went back down to room ten with the others. When she got back Trudy was talking about what she wanted to do with some of the money.

Trudy told them that she was glad Arleen left the room because you won't want to bring her with you if you decide to do this for me anyway.

"What is it that you want us to do next?" Erica asked.

A

She told them that her and her late husband use to go spend the weekend in Chicago, every once in a while. They would go shopping, out to eat and to shows. She told them when you walk the streets in Chicago people come up and just ask for handouts. "And as you can guess, because you know the kind of person I was that I didn't take to kindly to that."

She told them that on several occasions she was downright mean and cussed these homeless people out and told them to go get a job. So she asked the four of them if they would go to Chicago one of these weekends and they can make it like a mini vacation. They can use her money and get a hotel and go to shows and eat. But she wanted them to spend one whole day walking around the city and whenever they see anyone asking for a hand out she wanted them to take them in the nearest restaurant. Buy them a good meal and leave a good tip and tell the waitress to take good care of them. She wanted them to buy a nice meal for everyone who asks for help. She told them that she knows they need more than just a good meal and that they don't even have a place to live. "I don't have near enough money to give them all shelter but at least I can give them a good meal. I wish I was physically able to do this myself but I'm not so will you four do it for me?" she looked around the room.

Angie smiled and said, "That would be so much fun, I would love to do it. I was right about you when I was a teenager and I thought you were the classiest chick in the world."

"Can I tell you my other thing I would like to do with some of this money or am I overwhelming you guys?" Trudy looked around the table.

A

"What else, I can't wait to hear." Angie smiled and winked at Erica.

"I saw on the news about a month ago about a family whose house burnt down. Both parents and a little girl died when they were crushed under burning rubble when the front of the house caved in on them. Their 8 year old son's life was spared because he ran back to his bedroom to get his dog. The firemen were able to get him and his dog out through the window. The news showed the little boy holding his dog tight and crying his eyes out. Can you even imagine losing your whole family and your home gone at 8 years old? I wonder if you can find this little boy for me. I want to set up a college trust fund for him."

Erica said, "Let's count the money and see how much it is so we know how much you want to put in his trust fund."

"I was thinking $20,000. I like that number." Trudy laughed. "Go ahead count it if you want."

Erica and Angie opened the medal box and the shoe box and started counting. They counted $225,000 still in the shoe box. Just as they were closing the box Julie walked in with Arleen. "This gal can sing." Julie had her arm around Arleen. She didn't even notice or ask about the box.

"I lo-love it here. I w-want to move in h-h-ere. H-h-h-ow much does it cost Erica?" Arleen was so excited.

"I'll check into it for you Arleen." Erica replied. She knew it was very pricey.

Julie introduced herself to Tom and Angie and she stayed and visited

A

for a few minutes. Then she said, "I got to go take a crap," and out the door she went.

"She is s-s-s-o funny. I J-just love her. My daughter has been s-saying that she worries about me l-living alone. I'm going to a-ask her to p-p-put my house up for sale. Maybe with the money Trudy ju-just gave me and the money I g-get from my house, maybe I will have enough to l-l-ive here." She sounded so excited Erica didn't have the heart to tell her how expensive Sunset was.

"We better head on back to St. Louis. It has been a long weekend" Tom hugged Trudy, "Thank you so much for the gift. I think I am going to invest it for my retirement. I make a pretty good wage managing the restaurant but I need to put some money aside for the future."

"Well you know that is my specialty. If you want any advice about investing call me. I would love to help." Trudy wrote down her phone number and gave it to Tom.

Then Angie hugged Trudy and tears started down her face again, "Thank you Trudy, I'm so glad Erica found me. I was so bitter about what happened over 20 years ago, and I understand now. I never thought about what it was like to walk in your shoes."

"I have no excuse for treating you the way I did." Trudy grabbed some Kleenex and handed them to Angie. They hugged again.

Then Arleen said, "Group hug!" and she wrapped her arms around Angie and Trudy.

A

Erica used her key and let them out the back door. Then her and Nick told Trudy they need to go too. Trudy pointed to the medal box on the table, "Take this home and put it in a safe place."

Erica said, "I will do some checking and see if I can find out some information on that little boy and ill figure out a time that we can take that trip with Tom and Angie to Chicago.

Trudy asked them if they would also try to find out how much they can get for the coins and the jewelry and if they find someone to give them a good price to go ahead and sell them.

Erica let Nick out the back door with the box and she went out the front door to get her car that was still parked out front and then drove around back and picked up Nick and they headed home. All the way home they talked about what an exciting weekend it had been. "I cannot believe that we were just given twenty thousand dollars." Erica shouted with joy.

Nick said, "I think we should pay off our cars with this money."

"You don't think we should invest it for our future like Tom is doing?"

"I don't know. We both have a car payment and every month you get all uptight about money because with the mortgage and the car payments there just isn't anything left. We always make it but it is so tight. If we pay the cars off, that would give us $600 extra every month."

"We could do that and maybe put like 400 every month in savings and have 200 extra every month." They discussed it all the way home.

Tom and Angie talked all the way back to St. Louis. Arleen slept in the

A

back seat the whole time.

Angie said that she hoped to use the money from Trudy to get her brother in rehab. Tom said, "You know that there are some rehab centers that are free. They are usually Christian and get the money from charity."

"I know, my brother has already been to two charity ran rehab centers. They helped him for a while but then he went right back to using drugs. I'm hoping if I pay twenty thousand dollars for him to get him in rehab he will have a better chance staying off drugs. I don't know if twenty thousand is enough to get him in the best but I'm hoping it is."

Angie asked Tom if he would hold on to her money overnight for her. She said she didn't want to have that much cash on her if her brother would come over. It was Sunday and she wouldn't be able to go to the bank until tomorrow.

"You can stay at my house tonight and I will take you to work in the morning."

"Thank you but I really want to get home and get some things done before work tomorrow."

"I am kind of worried about leaving you there by yourself, with your brother breaking in and all."

"He wouldn't hurt me. He just wants money for drugs or food and if I don't have any he leaves."

"Sometimes people on drugs do things they wouldn't normally do. I just don't feel good about leaving you there, please stay at my house."

A

Angie assured him that she would be fine. They decided that Tom would leave work tomorrow at lunch time and pick Angie up at her work and take her to her bank so she could safely deposit the money. "Mondays are our slow day at work and I shouldn't have any trouble leaving early. Then I would like to take you out to lunch."

Angie looked in the back seat. "I guess she is sound asleep or she would have objected." Angie said looking at Arleen. They both laughed.

They talked and laughed and flirted all the way to St. Louis. They stopped At Arleen's place first. After they got her in the house and said their good byes. Tom asked Angie if she was sure she didn't want to stay at his house for the night.

"Please trust me I will be fine. My brother would for sure take that money if he knew I had it but he wouldn't hurt me."

So Tom brought her home and then he want home. Tom thought about Angie all the way home. In fact he thought about her all evening and he couldn't get to sleep that night because he was still thinking about her.

Angie cleaned up all the mess her brother had made and then took a long bath. As she lay in the bath she thought about Tom. I wonder if he likes me. When she got out of the bath she tried on all of her black pants looking in the mirror trying to decide which ones look the best on her. The maid uniform that she had worn to dig up the grave that morning is the uniform that she used to have to wear to work about 5 years ago. Now they just wear black pants and a black shirt. After she decided which pants

A

she was going to wear tomorrow she started trying on shirts. She normally wears a men's black T shirt. She had bought a package of 5 of them on sale about a year ago and she usually wears them every day. But she picked out a silky black button up blouse to wear tomorrow. She laid out her cloths for the morning and hopped into bed.

As Angie lay in bed thinking about tomorrow, she started thinking am I being silly. He doesn't like me, he is just being a nice guy. I need to quit getting my hopes up and get to sleep. She had a really hard time getting to sleep thinking about all that happened that day. She had decided to put all of the money in a savings account and start checking into how much it would cost to put her brother in a really good rehab center. That is if she could ever even get him to go. She finally dosed off.

Erica found the news story on the internet about the boy whose life was saved because he went back to get his dog, when their house was on fire. His parents and sister had died in the fire. The story didn't say who the boy was going to live with now that he lost his parents so Erica didn't know who to call to find out where the boy is now. So she called the news station that had reported the story and told them that she wanted to set up a college trust fund for that little boy and asked if they knew how to get a hold of whoever is his guardian. They said they would try to find something out and get back with her. They asked for her e mail address and told her that they would probably get back to her by an e mail.

The next day at work Erica was rushing to get everyone to breakfast so she could go talk to Trudy. Of course nobody was cooperating. Julie was bugging her to sing one song with her before breakfast. Erica decided it

A

would be quicker to sing a song than to try and talk her out of it. So they sang 'you got to get up every morning with a smile on your face' by Carole King. Before they finished the golden girls came in the room and joined them. Then Betty was like start it over we want to sing that again so they sang it again. Then as they walked down to the café for breakfast they told everyone they saw to put a smile on their face and show the world all the love in their hearts.

Erica went to get a tray to take to Ada and she got bad news that Ada was still in the hospital and it doesn't look good for her.

Page was still asleep when Erica peeked in on her, "do you want me to just bring you a tray today?"

"No, I want to go down to the café."

So Erica helped her to get dressed. "I can't believe you slept through all of that singing coming from Julie's room"

"Oh darn, did I miss out on a singing party this morning?" Page and Julie were getting to be good friends.

"Don't worry; I'm sure there will be more singing this afternoon." They got the rest of the lady's and all walked down to breakfast together.

As Erica walked down the hall with Trudy's breakfast tray she had a smile on her face thinking about how everyone in her isle were all getting along so well and becoming such good friends.

Trudy couldn't believe that Erica had already found the story about the little boy and called to try to get the information on him. Erica told her A they were going to call me back or e mail me as soon as they find anything out.

Then Trudy said, "I think Angie and Tom like each other."

"You noticed that too? Nick and I were talking about that last night. We think they make a cute couple."

"But Angie better watch out because Arleen has her eye on him too." Trudy laughed.

"I'm going to call Angie when I get home from work tonight and see if Tom asked her out on a date or if any hanky panky happened on their way home."

"Will you call me after you talk to her and fill me in on any gossip?" Trudy said excitedly.

"I will call you after I talk to Angie. If there is any gossip to tell."

When Erica got home from work that evening she wanted to call Angie and ask about her and Tom but she didn't know how to say it. She didn't really know Angie all that well but after the weekend they just spent together she felt like they were good friends.

She wanted to call her before Nick got home, so she just picked up the phone and dialed, not knowing what she would say. So when Angie answered she just said, "hi Angie it's me Erica."

Angie acted so excited to talk to her. "Hey how are you guys doing?"

"Good, I was just calling to make sure you all made it home safe and

A

everything."

"Yes we got home fine. Today Tom and I went out to lunch."

"Really" Erica tried to sound surprised.

"Well, I asked him to hold on to my money for me over night because it was Sunday and I didn't want to have all of that cash in my house incase my brother came over. So he kept it for me and then he picked me up from work on my lunch break and took me to the bank so I could deposit it in my account. Then we went to a Mexican restaurant and had lunch together."

Erica said, "I think he likes you Angie."

"I hope he does, I really like him. He is so nice and I can't tell if he likes me or if he is just being nice to me because he is just super nice."

"Did he ask you out for another date or anything?" Erica asked

"No after we had lunch he just took me back to my work and I was really late getting back so I just jumped out of the car and rushed back to work. Hay hold on a minute Erica, Tom is trying to call me."

"OK I'll hold on." Erica put dinner on the stove and put a load of laundry in the wash while she was on hold. Finally Angie switched back over to Erica.

"Are you still there Erica?"

"Yes I'm here. What did he say?"

A

"He said he had a nice time having lunch with me and he asked if I would go out to dinner with him on Wednesday evening."

"You said yes, didn't you?"

"Of course I did. I'm so excited, maybe he does like me."

"I told you he did. Boy Arleen is going to be so jealous." Erica laughed. "While you guys are out Wednesday night talk to him about when would be a good time for both of you guys to go to Chicago? Nick and I are free about every weekend."

"I am really looking forward to that. I will ask Tom when he wants to go and I will get back to you."

"OK great then I'll talk to you on Thursday or Friday,"

"Good bye."

Nick got home from work just as Erica hung up the phone and she was so excited to tell him that Angie and Tom went on a date and that they have another one planned for Wednesday. As soon as her and Nick finished eating dinner Erica called Trudy to tell her about Angie and Tom going on a date and already having another one planned. Trudy was even more excited than Erica about it.

After Erica took her shower and was relaxing for the night she noticed she had an email from the news station saying that the little boy she had questioned them about was in foster care and they gave her an email address for the adoption agency that was handling his case. Erica sent an email to the adoption agency and told them that someone wants

A

to set up a college trust fund for that little boy and she needs some information about the little boy to get it started.

While Erica was on her computer sending the emails Nick was on his looking for a good place to take Trudy's jewelry and coins to get an appraisal on them. He found a place close by so he told Erica he would be a little late tomorrow evening. He would take the jewelry and coins tomorrow after work and get them appraised.

The work week seemed to go by so fast for Erica. The lady's at Sunset nursing home section C were all starting to get along so well and have a lot of fun together. Julie taught all the other lady's how to play a dice game that she had learned from her grandmother. Every morning after breakfast they would all sing karaoke in Julie's karaoke Christmas room. Then after lunch they would all play grandma's game in the lounge. Trudy sang with them a couple times and she played the dice game too. Ada still hadn't come back; she was still in the hospital.

Angie called Erica on Thursday evening and told her all about her date with Tom. Angie said "We had a lot of fun. We went out to dinner and then we went bowling. He is such a great guy."

"Is he a great kisser?" Erica questioned

"He did give me a little kiss good night. But I will need some more samples to know if he is a great kisser." Angie laughed.

They made plans to go the weekend after next to Chicago and buy dinner for homeless people, with Trudy's money.

A

Nick took the coins and jewelry to the pawn shop for an appraisal and the coins were worth exactly what Trudy said they were worth. The guy studied the jewelry very carefully. Nick told him it use to belong to an actress but he wasn't sure who. The guy said he would get back to him on a price for the jewelry.

A

Chapter fourteen

Erica got a phone call from the adoption agency and they asked what all information she needed to get that trust fund set up. Trudy had told her that she would need his full legal name and his social security number and his guardians name's and address. They emailed Erica the foster parents address and phone number and said she should just send them the forms. It turned out that the little boy only lived about 45 minutes away.

When Erica told Trudy she was going to send a form to the foster parents Trudy ask her if she would go there herself with the form and find out if the foster parents were planning to adopt the boy. "If they are not going to adopt, then we will wait till he is in a permanent home before we set up the trust fund. That would be easier than changing everything when he gets a permanent home."

So Erica and Nick called the foster parents and asked if they could meet with them on Saturday. Erica couldn't believe how much time Nick was putting into doing all of this stuff for Trudy. But it seemed like it was making their love for each other grow and their marriage stronger. They never seemed to be bored anymore. Nick hadn't even wanted to go to the bar.

The drive to go meet the little boy and his foster parents was a little stressful because it was raining so hard you could barely see out the windows. Then it started to hail. Nick pulled off the interstate and under cover at a gas station. "I just payed this car off, I don't want to get hail damage." He got out and examined the car. It looked fine so he got back

A

in the car and they sat there for 5 minutes waiting for the hail to stop.

While they were sitting there Erica smiled at Nick and said, "I am amazed at how you just agreed to make this trip today and at all the time you are putting into helping Trudy."

"I am having fun. I always thought it would be great to have a lot of money and be able to just help people and I am getting to do it but with someone else's money. Besides that the lady gave us $20,000. Nick said as he pulled out of the gas station. "The hail stopped, I just hope it doesn't start up again."

"I am really looking forward to next weekend because it will be a lot of fun to have a getaway for us and it will be fun to buy hungry people meals."

"Me too, I really like Angie and Tom. I think it will be a great time." Nick said and he grabbed Erica's hand and held it as they drove down the interstate.

When they finally found the address they were looking for they were a half an hour late. The foster parents were a sweet old couple but they looked like they might be in their seventies. They invited Erica and Nick in and offered them some ice tea. Erica explained to them that a lady at her work saw the story on the news about the fire and the little boy being alive because he went back to get his dog. After seeing the story she wanted to open a college trust fund for the little boy.

"Are you planning to adopt him?" Erica asked.

A

The women motioned for them to come on out on the front porch. "I don't want him to hear us talking." She said when they got out on the porch. "Jason is not handling all of this very well; he stays in his room all day and will hardly talk or eat."

"I can't even imagine. Poor little guy. This is a lot for him to have to deal with. Is he getting professional help?" Erica asked.

"Yes someone has been coming three times a week to talk to him. I am just glad it is summer break because there is no way he could be going to school right now." The woman answered.

"Doesn't he have any grandparents, uncles or aunts to take him in?" Nick asked.

"Well he has grandparents but they are in poor health. He has an aunt whom I met at the funeral. She apparently lives in California and is a single mother with three of her own children and is struggling financially. When they brought him to me on the night of the fire, I thought we would just have him for a few days. We assumed that the aunt from California would take him as soon as she got here but since she cannot take him he is still here."

"Are you planning to adopt him?" Erica asked.

"Oh goodness no! We are much too old. We have children and grandchildren of our own. We are just short term foster parents. The adoption agency is trying to find him a permanent home but because he is eight years old it is hard to find. Everyone wants baby's or at least kids less than 3 years old. I'm thinking that this trust fund is really great news. A

It might help him find a home if he comes with college already paid for."

"Here is my phone number. Will you please call me when he finds a permanent home and then we will get the trust fund set up? The donor wants his guardians to be the beneficiary, so it will be easier to wait till he is placed in a permanent home than to redo everything when he is." Erica handed her a piece of paper with her phone number on it.

"Of course, I'll call you but it may take a while with his age."

"Can I meet him?" Erica asked.

"Sure, but he won't talk to you." They all walked back in the house and the women showed her to Jason's room.

Nick waited in the living room with the couple while Erica went in the bed room and introduced herself to Jason. "Hi Jason, my name is Erica."

Jason was sitting on the floor with his dog. Erica went over and sat on the floor with them. "This dog is lucky to have you. I hear that you saved his life."

"But I couldn't save my mom's life."

"I know, I am so sorry Jason. This has to be so hard for you." Erica wasn't sure what to say.

"My mom and dad and sister are in heaven now."

"You are right they are in heaven and you will see them again one day." Erica hoped she was saying the right thing.

A

"I want to go there now."

"Then who would take care of your dog?" Erica said holding back tears.

"Buster could go there too."

"I know this is so hard for you but if your mom and dad could talk to you right now they would tell you to live your life and they will be there waiting for you when you are old and you will have eternity together."

The little boy started to cry. Erica didn't know what to do. She just scooted over to him and put her arms around him and said, "It will be ok buddy. Hang in there." The dog climbed up on Jason's lap and licked him on the face. Jason laughed. She sat and talked to him about his dog for a few minutes and then she said, "I have to go now. You hang in there." Erica got up and walked out of the room and down the hall. She turned around and saw little Jason peeking out of the bed room door watching her walk away.

"I heard him talking to you in there; I can't believe it because I haven't heard him say but a few words the whole time he has been here."

Erica smiled, "Well we better go. Please call me if you hear any news on a permanent placement for him."

They thanked them for their time and for the ice tea and walked out to the car. As soon as Nick pulled away Erica said, "I want to adopt Jason."

Nick drove around the corner and pulled over. He told Erica he was thinking the same thing. "Get on the internet and find an address for the

A

adoption agency and let's go there right now."

Erica screamed and hugged Nick so hard. As she searched the internet for an address she was shaking so hard she could hardly hold her phone. She found the address and phone number and she tried to call them but got an answering machine. "I guess they are not in the office on the weekend."

"You can call them on Monday." Nick started toward home.

"Do you think we should go back and tell the foster parents?"

"I think maybe we should just think about it for the weekend and then call them on Monday." Nick said as he pulled onto the interstate.

"I have never been so sure about anything in my life. I don't need to think about it." Erica said with tears running down her cheeks. She looked over at Nick wondering if he was going to start listing reasons why they should think about it.

"Then let's make it happen. Call them on Monday and find out what we have to do to get the process started."

They talked the whole way home about how it will be having an eight year old living with them. Nick said, "Trudy has made me realize that doing things for others makes me feel better than doing things for myself. We don't have a lot of money like Trudy, but I think we can give this little boy a good home. I think you would be a great mother."

They both agreed that ever since the day Trudy asked them to help her, their life has been an adventure. If they are able to adopt Jason it will

A

be the biggest adventure of all. Erica called Trudy and told her the good news.

When they got home they spent the whole evening on the internet reading about adoption. They learned that one of the qualifications was to have a home suitable for the child. They decided to spend Sunday cleaning out the extra bed room. They already had a bed and a dresser in there but the dresser was full of Erica's winter clothes and the closet was full of junk. In the middle of the room on the floor was a piece of cardboard with a half done puzzle that Erica started months ago and never finished. They put the puzzle back in the box. Erica put all of her winter clothes in plastic totes and put them in the basement. They went through all of the stuff under the bed and in the closet and filled the car with bags to take to good will. They took the rest of the stuff to the basement. One of the things they found under the bed was Nick's old super Nintendo. Nick started hooking up his Nintendo to the down stairs TV and Erica started cleaning up the basement. "We should get a ping pong table. That would be a fun family thing we could do." Erica said excitedly.

Nick replied, "Our back yard has a perfect place for a basketball goal."

Then they both collapsed on the sofa in the basement and laughed. "We are getting ahead of ourselves."

"It's getting late. Let's order pizza and watch a little TV. If we don't take our minds off of this, I am never going to be able to get to sleep tonight. Is pepperoni and mushroom good with you?" Erica said as she

A

picked up her phone.

They spent the whole evening eating pizza and playing super Mario in the basement.

At about 9:00 Angie called, "Is it too late to be calling?"

"No its fine what's up, is everything ok?"

"Yes everything is great. I spent the whole afternoon with Tom."

Erica walked up the steps so she could hear Angie better because super Mario music was blaring through the basement. "What did you guys do?"

"Well he had to work all day yesterday and this morning. So he picked me up at about noon. He took me to a park and we sat at a picnic table and ate McDonald's food and talked. The park had a lake with a side walk around it and so we walked around the lake and he held my hand most of the time. And the answer is yes."

"What are you talking about, the answer to what?"

"You asked me if he was a good kisser. The answer is yes!"

Erica screamed. "Oh my gosh!"

Nick came up the stairs and shook his head and said, "I'm going to bed."

The girls talked on the phone for over an hour. Angie talked about how much she really liked Tom. They both talked about looking forward

A

to going to Chicago next weekend.

"My brother hasn't broken into my house since that time you guys were here."

"That's good"

"I guess it's good. It makes me worry. What is he eating and where is he. I hope he isn't in jail again or what if he is dead."

"If he were in jail or dead you would have gotten a phone call. Maybe he got a job and is taking care of himself."

"Ya right!"

Erica tried to change the subject, "I got to tell you some really great news. We went to meet the foster parents of that little boy yesterday. So we could talk to them about the trust fund." Erica was so excited that she screamed, "Me and Nick want to adopt him!"

"Wow that is fantastic. I can't believe you let me go on and on about my date and my brother when you had this big news."

"When I met the little guy I fell in love with him and immediately I wanted to adopt him but I couldn't believe it when Nick said he wants too. I'm so excited."

"I'm so happy for you guys."

"We are going to call the agency in the morning and try to get the

A

process started. We have been cleaning and organizing our house all weekend, trying to get ready for this." Erica looked over at the clock. "I could talk about this all night but I better get to bed."

They talked a little more about the trip to Chicago next weekend. Erica finally got off the phone and got the coffee pot ready for in the morning and climbed into bed around 11:00 but she didn't fall asleep till about midnight thinking about everything that is happening all because of Miss Trudy.

The alarm went off the next morning and before either of them was out of bed the doorbell rang. Nick slipped on some pants and went to the door rubbing his eyes. A police officer was standing there when he opened the door. Erica peeked out the window in her room to see who it was and when she saw the police car in the drive way she ran down the hall in her robe. They both stood at the door still only half awake asking is everything all right?

"Are you Nick Probps?"

"Yes sir."

"Did you try to pawn some jewelry last week?"

"I took some jewelry in to have it appraised."

"The jewelry you brought to that shop to be appraised was reported stolen about a year or so ago. I'm afraid I'm going to have to take you down to the station."

Nick and Erica started talking at the same time. They tried to tell him

A

that they were getting it apprised for a friend, but the officer said he had to take Nick to the station for questioning and that everything he said needed to be recorded.

"Do you still have the jewelry?"

"Yes."

"Then I need you to give it to me and we will hold onto it at the station until this is resolved." Then he told Erica she needed to call a lawyer.

Nick asked if he could put on a shirt and some shoes and he told Erica to call Trudy and ask her to call her son. It was probably her son who reported it as stolen. Nick left in the cop car and Erica called Trudy and then drove to the police station.

At the station they questioned Nick and then told him he was free to go. He wasn't under arrest yet. They said if his story doesn't check out he will be arrested. They said they needed to question the person who reported the jewelry stolen and they also wanted to question Trudy.

Erica drove Nick home and they both ended up being late for work. When Erica got to work she rushed everyone down to breakfast and then she rushed to Trudy's room without even getting her breakfast tray. "Did you call your son?"

"Yes I called and told him that I asked Nick to take that jewelry in to be appraised and that Nick didn't steal it. And I told him to call the police station right away. Is Nick in jail?"

A

"No they just questioned him and let him go for now. If your son calls them and tells them that Nick didn't steal it I think everything will be ok." Erica sighed. "If Nick would get arrested we will not be able to adopt Jason." She started to cry.

"He is not going to be arrested. That is my jewelry to do what I please with. Tell that cop to come and talk to me." Trudy said with authority.

"He said he was going to come question you."

"GOOD! Now where is my breakfast? All of this drama has made me hungry."

Erica laughed, "I'll go get your tray." She headed down the hall feeling much better. The other ladies were still eating and gabbing so Erica was able to get Trudy's tray and head right back to her room. She set the tray on the table and both of them sat down to eat breakfast.

"Do the police know about the coins or the money?" Trudy asked.

"No they never asked us about the coins, I guess your son didn't report them stolen."

"Good if my son finds out you have the coins or any cash he will want that too." She took a bite of her bagel and just then the door opened and a distinguished looking man walked in. For a second Erica though he was probably a police detective here to question Trudy.

Then he said, "Mom, how did you have that jewelry? I brought all of your belongings here and unpacked them myself. You did not have that

A

jewelry when you moved in here. I reported it stolen."

Erica realized it was Trudy's son and he sounded mad. So she sat quiet and let Trudy do the talking.

"I hid that jewelry because you were selling all of my stuff and I wanted to keep that." Trudy stood up and crossed here arms.

"All you had to do is say you wanted it and I would have packed it for you."

"That is not true and you know it. That jewelry is worth a lot of money and you wanted to sell it."

"Mom, I asked you about it a few days before the sale and you said you didn't know where it was so I assumed someone stole it. Now who is this guy that was trying to pawn it?"

Erica spoke up, "Hi, my name is Erica. I work here and Miss Trudy asked me to find out what the jewelry was worth. My husband wasn't trying to pawn it. He was just getting an appraisal for Trudy. This morning the police showed up at our house and took him down to the police station for questioning."

Trudy's son said, "Well, I am sorry for your trouble. Can I please speak to my mother alone?"

Erica started to get up but Trudy looked her in the eye and yelled, "SIT! I want her in here. You can say anything to me in front of her. She is my friend."

A

Her son Michael, looked over at Erica and then back at his mom. "They could have easily taken that jewelry somewhere and pawned it and got a lot of money and you would have never seen them again. It's the darn good thing that I had reported it stolen."

"Now you listen here. I am a good judge of character and this girl and her husband care more about me than you and your kids do." Trudy sat down at the table next to Erica.

"How can you say that mom? I am your son and I love you and so do your grandkids and great grandkids. This girl just works for you."

"When was the last time you were here for a visit? I can't even remember when it was. But boy that jewelry is mentioned and here you are. All you and my grandkids ever cared about was my money."

"This girl works here mom for money. And she is pretending to be a friend hoping for money."

"Is that why she has spent her last three weekends, helping me?" Trudy put her arm around Erica. You hardly ever even call and I haven't seen you in months. This girl does things for me on her days off and she even calls me on her days off work."

Then Michael sat down. He put his head in his hands. "Mom there is something I need to tell you. I am sorry I haven't been here to visit. The last couple of months have been rough. Little Winnie ran away. She dropped out of school and left and we haven't heard a thing from her. We have been searching all over for her. I knew if I came here or called you that you would notice something was wrong. We didn't want to upset

A

you."

Trudy looked over at her son and could see that he was truly worried about his granddaughter. "I'm sorry son; I can't imagine how worried Bill and Judy must be. Winnie was here to see me but it's been close to 3 months ago."

Michael perked up, "Did she say anything to you about leaving home?"

"She told me that she was dropping out of college. I got the feeling she was wanting me to talk to her parents about it but then she never asked me too. She did not say anything about going anywhere."

"Are you sure it was three months ago? Time can probably go by slow in here. Maybe it just seems like three months ago." Michael asked.

Erica butted in; "We keep a log of all visitors here. Everyone signs in at the front desk. I will go get the books and we can see exactly when it was." She got up to leave the room.

"Thank you that would be really helpful to know." Michael nodded to Erica.

When Erica got back to the room with the last four months sign in books she sat down at the table and started to look through them. Michael came over to the table and sat down next to Erica and started to look through one of the books. He said to Erica, "Mother told me about how she wanted to sell the jewelry so that she will have money of her own to spend. She told me how she would like to use the money to do

A

good deeds. I think that is great but that jewelry is worth way too much money for her to have in this room or even in an account of her own. At her age people try to take advantage. It's just not safe. I'm thinking maybe I will give her an allowance and she can spend it on whatever she wants."

"I'm standing right here don't talk about me like I'm not in the room or like I am a child. I am not a child and I do not want allowance." Trudy sounded furious.

Michael stood up and yelled at his mother, "I can't believe you are acting like this when your great granddaughter is missing."

Erica tried to stop the yelling, "I found her signature. Winnie, its right here. Hum it looks like she was here on May 10th.

Michael looked at the book, "yes that's her signature. She has been missing since May 21st. The police found her car in St. Louis the beginning of June."

"What?" Trudy freaked out, "Her car was abandoned? Oh my lord, now I'm so worried. I just figured she wanted to get away for a while. But if she abandoned her car something is wrong." Trudy collapsed onto the sofa.

Michael went over and sat by his mom, "I didn't want to worry you mom, but it doesn't look good. I'm so sorry; I know how much you adore that little girl. We are not giving up hope. We have called all of her friends. We have hired two of the best private investigators."

"Was her car broke down when they found it?" Trudy asked.

A

'It was left parked on the side of a road in St louis with a flat tire. She had a suitcase full of clothes in the trunk and her purse was never found. The last time her credit card was used was May 21, for a tank of gas." Michael looked sadly at his mom and started to cry.

They both held each other sobbing. Erica wished there was something she could do. Michael stood up and Erica handed him a box of Kleenex. "I know this is hard mom but we can't give up hope. All we can do now is pray. This whole thing has got us all going to church and we have a whole big congregation praying for Winnie."

Trudy had tears running down her cheeks. She looked at Erica and said, "This weekend will you take me to St. Louis to drive around and look for her."

Before Erica could say anything Michael said, "No mom. That will not do any good. We have the police and two very good private detectives trying to find her. You just stay here and pray." Then he looked at Erica and said, "I can see that my mom really trusts you, so I trust you too. I will call the police station and drop the charges against your husband and ask them to give the jewelry back to him. If you guys don't mind just hold onto it for a while. Please don't sell it to that pawn shop. I want to make sure that my mom gets a good price for it. After we find Winnie, I will help you find the right buyer for it and my mom can use the money for whatever she wants."

"Thank you for dropping the charges." Erica smiled at Michael.

He gave his mom one more hug and with tears in his eyes he said,

A

"Please mom, I don't want to have to worry about you. You just stay here and pray. I don't want you going up to St. Louis looking for her and then you go missing and I will have to send out private eyes looking for you. Stay put!" Then he looked at Erica, "I know she can be persuasive, don't let her talk you into that. She needs to stay here."

Erica promised him that she wouldn't take Trudy out of the care center. Then to her surprise before he left he gave Erica a hug and told her thank you for taking such good care of his mom.

"I love you mom, I have to go. I will call you if we hear anything at all about Winnie. You just keep praying." And he hugged his mom and walked out the door.

"Are you ok Trudy, do you want me to go get you a fresh tray of breakfast?"

"No I don't feel much like eating. I want to be alone." Trudy climbed into her bed.

"I understand. I'll take this tray and bring you a snack later. I need to go check on the other gal's anyway." Erica walked out of Trudy's room and found the golden girls checking out Trudy's son's butt as he walked down the hall. "You girls are nothing but trouble." Erica joked with them.

"We have a big game of charades starting in a little bit do you think Trudy would want to play? We are all meeting in the lounge in ten minutes. Almost everyone from C is going to play. I'll go and ask Trudy." Betty started to go in Trudy's room.

A

"No Betty, we need to leave Trudy alone right now. She is upset about something and wants to be alone. You girls go ahead and go to the lounge. Does Miss Page want to play?"

"I think so." Betty answered.

"I will help Page get to the lounge and then I will go make some punch and snacks to bring to you all.

While everyone was playing charades and Trudy was napping, Erica called Nick to tell him that it was Trudy's son that reported the jewelry stolen and that he was dropping charges. Nick was busy at work and couldn't talk long so she couldn't tell him about her granddaughter till she got home that night.

Over dinner she told Nick about Trudy's great granddaughter missing. Nick couldn't believe that Erica didn't call the adoption agency to get started on adopting Jason. "It all you talked about yesterday. You kept saying I can't wait to call them. Then you didn't call them."

"I'm sorry but you got arrested this morning. I thought it would be best to wait till that was all cleared up."

"I guess you're right, I am just excited about it. I wasn't even worrying about the arrest all day I just kept thinking about having a son."

Erica hugged Nick "Aww, I am so glad that you are excited about it too. I will call them in the morning. I wonder if we should call the police station to make sure this is all straightened out or if they will get a hold of us?" before the words were out of her mouth the doorbell rang.

A

An officer was standing there with a box in his hand, "Are you Nick Probps?"

"Yes sir I am." Nick answered.

"All charges against you were dropped and I was told to return this to you. I just need you to sign this release form." The officer handed Nick a clip board and he signed.

The officer left and they set the box on the coffee table and opened it up and looked at the jewelry. "I can't believe this is worth so much. We better find a good place to hide it until Trudy's son helps us sell it. If it is worth so much money and a lot of people know we have it now. I don't want to just leave it in your top drawer."

"I have a great idea. Let's wait till after dark and burry it in our back yard and put a stone marked Goldie on top of it." Erica rubbed her hands together, thinking about how clever she thought herself to be.

They didn't have a metal box so they put it in a jar and after dark they buried it in their back yard. Erica found a small flat rock and wrote Goldie on it with a permanent marker.

A

Chapter fifteen

The next morning Erica called the adoption agency that was handling Jason's foster care. She was able to talk to the same women that she spoke with last week about the trust fund. She told her that after meeting Jason they have decided that they would love to adopt him. The woman was thrilled. "It is very hard to place a child his age. Here at this agency we have 6 older children needing permanent homes and we are a small town. Bigger cities have even more older children needing homes." She told her that if her and Nick want to first apply to be Jason's foster parents they will be able to have him sooner and then they can start the adoption procedure.

She said that the foster parents who have him now are much too old and they call the agency almost every day asking how much longer they will have him. So she was very happy about the news and she sent Erica all of the forms to get started.

That night her and Nick spent the whole evening getting all of the paper work finished up and they e-mailed the forms back to the agency.

On Friday before Erica left work for the weekend she asked Trudy if she was sure she still wanted them to go to Chicago. "With your granddaughter missing I thought maybe you would want us to postpone the trip."

"No I want you all to go. Call me over the weekend and let me know how it is going. I want to hear all about it."

So Nick and Erica got up super early on Saturday and headed to St.

A

Louis. They drove straight to Tom's house and made good time they got to his house about 8:00 am and they all got in Tom's SUV and headed over to pick up Angie. She was all ready to go when they got to her place. She jumped in the car and said how excited she was about this trip. She had never been to Chicago before. Before they pulled away Angie's phone rang.

Angie sounded very upset. "What did you do now?" Then a few minutes later she said, "OH MY GOD!" Then they heard her say, "What modular home are you talking about, why why what? I don't know what modular home you are talking about." Then a minute later she said, "I have money I will get you a lawyer."

After she got off the phone she told them all to go on without her. She told them that her brother was in a lot of trouble and he needs her help. She got out of the car and went toward her house. They all got out of the car and went after her.

"We are not going to Chicago without you Angie. What's going on with your brother?" Tom asked. They all went into Angie's living room. Angie was crying and it was hard to understand her but she told them that her brother said a friend talked him into robbing a liquor store. The friend had a gun and a car. He told her brother to go in the store and rob them at gun point and he would be right down the road a little bit waiting with the getaway car. When her brother tried to hold the clerk up with the gun, the clerk pulled out a gun so her brother shot him and ran out of the store and his friend took off without him when he heard the shots fired. So he got picked up by the police walking down the road. He is denying

A

everything to the cops but the store had cameras.

Tom said, "Angie there is nothing you can do for your brother. He is going to have to face his punishment for the crime. Is the guy he shot dead?"

Angie got mad at Tom and asked them all to leave. She started screaming at all of them saying that they just don't understand. They didn't leave and they finally got Angie to calm down.

Erica said to Angie, "I know you planned to use your money from Trudy to help your brother get off drugs. But if you use it to get him a lawyer you might as well just throw it away. If the store has cameras he is going to be found guilty and no lawyer will be able to help him. Maybe if he spends some time in prison he will get the help he needs to stop doing drugs and straighten up."

"Erica is right." Tom said, "Maybe prison is the best place for him."

"He has been in prison lots of times already. It never helped him before. He told me drugs were easy to come by in prison. So he will probably be worse when he gets out and every time he gets out he is meaner too." She sobbed.

Tom hugged her and Erica sat on the other side of her rubbing her leg. Angie kept on telling them all too please go on to Chicago and have a good time. She didn't want their weekend ruined because of her brother. They all refused to go. "We will reschedule the trip to Chicago."

"I need to go to the police station and ask them more questions. My

A

brother only had a limited amount of time; I want to know more details. I don't even know if he killed the store clerk or not."

"We will take you sweetheart." Tom comforted her.

Then Nick asked her, "What was your brother saying about a modular home at the end of your conversation?"

Angie looked up at Nick, "OH ya, he said something about for me to go check the modular home that is in a ditch in the back of my trailer park. I really didn't know what he was talking about."

"Is there a modular home in a ditch in the back of this trailer park?" Nick asked.

Angie answered, "I don't even know. There is like a junk yard with a bunch of old trailer parts and stuff."

"Let's go check it out." Nick said to Tom.

Angie said, "He probably put some drugs in there or maybe some pot plants. Let's don't worry about that right now. I just want to go try to see my brother and talk to the police."

"I don't think they are going to let you see him."

"Well I still want to go talk to the police and find out what exactly happened." She picked up her purse and started toward the door. "I really wish you all would just go to Chicago. I can take a cab to the police station. I'm fine I just need to be here for my brother."

Tom said, "We will take you." They all went out and got back in Toms

A

SUV.

Nick said to Tom, "Just drive to the back of this subdivision first. I just want to look for the modular home in a ditch and check it out."

Angie started to get all upset again because she just wanted to get to the police station and get some more information. Not knowing if her brother actually killed someone was making her upset. She snapped at Nick. Nick snapped back at her and told her, "Your brother told you to check it out. You keep on wanting to help him, well then you should do what he asked you to do."

Tom started to get into it with Nick telling him not to be harsh with Angie she is going through enough right now. But then Angie agreed maybe Nick was right and they should go look for the modular home in a ditch.

They drove back to where Angie knew there was a junk yard but it was only a bunch of stripped cars and trailer parts lying around with weeds grown up around everything. They got out of the car and looked around. Nick walked through the junk yard looking around and then he spotted a modular home in the woods a little ways off. It was half turned over into a ditch. He hollered to the others pointing to the woods. "There it is, let's go check it out."

They all started walking towards the woods. Tom said, "Everyone watch for snakes."

The door to the trailer was up in the air because of it being tipped half way over but there was an old seat out of a truck laying there that

A

you could climb on and reach the door. Nick climbed on the truck seat and opened the door and lifted himself up into the trailer. It was filthy dirty and smelled really bad. "Do you see anything?" Angie yelled from outside.

Tom looked around and yelled back, "No I only see a big mess and then he walked to the back of the trailer and yelled, "SHIT! Call 911."

The other three climbed up into the trailer. In the back of the trailer was a young girl handcuffed to a rail. She looked to be dead. Nick was bent over her and he yelled, "Call 911 right now! She is still breathing."

Erica ran back to the car to get her phone and called 911 and tried to give them directions to where they were at. Her heart was beating so fast she could hardly talk. It seemed like an hour but it was only like ten minutes when three police cars and an ambulance pulled up. Erica flagged them over to her and walked with them to the trailer in the woods. Luckily the police had something in their car to cut the handcuff off of the girl. They got her out of the trailer and put her on a stretcher and carried her to the ambulance and it pulled away with sirens blaring.

Angie tried to tell the others to not mention her brother in this because he is in enough trouble.

Nick said, "Sorry Angie, we have to tell the truth."

They gave the police all of the information they had and instead of going to the police station to find out about Angie's brother they all went straight to the hospital to find out how the girl was.

The girl did not have any identification on her and the police didn't find anything in the trailer that would give them any leads on who she was. One of the officers that came to the hospital was asking Angie more questions. She really didn't have any information to tell them. She told the truth that her brother told them to check out the old modular home and that is how they found the girl but that she had no idea who she might be. The officer told them that he was going to go back to the station and go through his missing person reports and try to figure out who this girl is.

All at once Erica gasp, "Could this be Trudy's great granddaughter?"

The cop asked, "Who is Trudy?"

Erica tried to tell him but he was getting more confused. He got out his phone and called the station and asked about a missing girl named Winnie.

The doctor came out and asked if Angie was family? The officer said, "She is a Jane Doe. Is she going to be all right?"

The doctor said she was starving to death and had severe dehydration. She slipped into a coma from the dehydration. They are pumping fluids in her and feeding her intravenously but only time will tell.

"I'm calling Trudy." Erica got out her phone.

"You will get her hopes up. Just wait till we know more." Nick urged.

"I need to ask her what Winnie looks like. I need to call her." She dialed the phone.

A

When Trudy answered she said in a happy voice, "Are you already in Chicago?"

Erica started thinking maybe Nick was right she shouldn't have called. But she did call so she tried to get to the point. "We are in a hospital in St. Louis and there is a girl here who is about Winnie's age and I was just wondering if you could tell me what Winnie looks like."

Trudy got excited and started asking all kinds of questions. Erica told her, "I will tell you the details later just tell me what she looks like and if there is anything about her that could help identify her."

Trudy answered, "She has light brown hair and green eyes. Her hair is long and wavy. She is very thin. She is beautiful."

Erica thought about the girl that just got carried out of that trailer on a stretcher and she didn't look beautiful. She was skin and bones, her hair all matted with feces and urine all over her. "Does she have a birthmark or anything?"

"Yes, she has a tattoo on her shoulder. It's a peace sign."

The doctor was still talking to the police officer. Erica said, "Hold on Trudy." She went over and interrupted the doctor and asked him if the girl had a peace sign tattoo on her shoulder.

The doctor said, "Yes she does."

"It's Winnie." Erica couldn't believe it.

"Who is Winnie?" The officer and Angie both asked.

A

Erica put up her hand the way Trudy always does. She told Trudy I think we found Winnie. Call your son and tell him to come to Christian hospital in St. Louis right away. After she got off the phone with Trudy, she explained to Angie and to the cop about Trudy's missing granddaughter having a peace sign tattoo and being about 20 years old.

Angie was not taking all of this very well. She knew her brother had to have handcuffed the girl there and he just shot someone else. She had had so much hope that with the money Trudy gave her she was going to help her brother get straightened out an now he was in more trouble than ever. And if this is Trudy's great granddaughter and her brother causes her to die. Angie had all of this going through her head. The next thing she knew she was on the floor with Tom leaning over her saying Angie are you all right?

She had collapsed. The doctor got her up into a chair and a nurse brought her a drink of water. Tom said, "Do you want something to eat Angie?"

"No I can't eat right now. I'll be fine." Angie said in a shaky voice with tears in her eyes.

Tom went down to the cafeteria and got some snacks and soda's for everyone and brought them back to the waiting room. Everyone ate a little, except Angie but she did take a few sips of soda.

A couple hours later Michael walked into the waiting room. Erica spotted him and walked over to him and tried to explain how they found the girl in an abandoned trailer. She told him that she looks to be about

A

20 years old and she has a peace sign tattoo on her arm. Michael couldn't contain himself. Where is she? I need to see her."

They went up to the nurses station and asked the nurse if they could go in her room. Erica said, "This man may be her grandfather."

Erica and Michael walked into the room and Michael immediately knew it was his little Winnie. He ran to her and touched her face and kissed her forehead and started crying like a baby. The doctor came into the room. "Is she going to be all right, doctor?" Michael asked.

The doctor answered, "We will have to wait to see. I don't think she would have lived through the day if she hadn't been found today. She was on the brink of starvation and severely dehydrated. We are hoping with nourishment she will regain conciseness and hopefully there will be no brain damage. Time will tell."

Michael started crying again. The police officer came to the door and said, "Can this man identify her?"

Erica answered, "Yes, she is his granddaughter."

"When he feels up to it, I need to ask him some questions." He walked away.

Erica looked over at Michael holding his granddaughters hand and sobbing. "I'll give you some time alone. She went out to the waiting room to find the officer questioning Angie about her brother's phone call this morning. Erica sat down by Nick and held his hand. "What a crazy day. I'm going to call Trudy and tell her that it is Winnie."

A

Erica dialed her phone. Trudy was so happy to hear that Winnie was found. Erica decided not to tell her what the doctor said about possible brain damage. Trudy asked if Michael had called Bill yet. Erica said, "I don't think he has yet. He is still in the room with Winnie."

"We need to let Bill and Judy know. I know they have been worried sick, they will want to be there."

"Let me go ask your son if he has called his son." Erica turned around and saw Michael was outside of Winnie's room on the phone. "Trudy, I see Michael on the phone right now I bet he is talking to Winnie's parents as we speak."

"They are going to be so thankful. We all need to be thanking God for this answered prayer." Trudy sounded so relieved.

"Well keep on praying Trudy; she is not out of the woods yet." Erica wasn't sure if she should have said that.

"I want to see her. Maybe Bill and Judy will pick me up on their way up to the hospital."

Erica told her that she would talk to Michael and call her back. Michael said that Bill and Judy were on their way. They are not going to want to stop and get mom. She needs to stay put. I will call her in a few minutes and talk to her. Then he asked how they ended up finding her in an abandoned trailer anyway and if they had any idea how she got there.

It was really hard for Angie but she told Trudy's son the whole story about how they had all met because of Trudy and how they were going to

A

go to Chicago and buy hungry people meals for Trudy. She told him that right when they were getting ready to leave for Chicago her phone rang and her brother was in jail and about him saying go and check the abandoned modular home in the back of your trailer park. She told him that she just wanted to get to the police station and talk to them about her brother and find out more information about what happened to land him in jail, but that Nick wanted to go see why he said to go check the abandoned modular home.

Angie said, "If they were not at my house I know for sure I would have never went and checked that old trailer. I really thought he wanted me to go get his drugs out of it or something. If it were not for Nick insisting that we go find the modular home my brother mentioned, we would not have found Winnie."

After she stopped talking they all sat in silence for a minute and then Michael said, "So if my mom hadn't asked you to find these two people so she could apologize to them for something that happened years ago, then you all would have never met. Angie would have been alone when she got the phone call from her brother and she wouldn't have gone to find the abandoned trailer and Winnie wouldn't have been found today. The doctor said she wouldn't have made it through the day if she hadn't been found today."

They all sat in silence again, then Erica spoke, "I think God had to have had a hand in all of this."

Nick said, "Amen."

A

Not to long later Winnie's parents arrived frantic. Michael showed them to Winnie's room.

Angie asked Tom if he would take her to the police station because she wanted to talk to them and find out what exactly happened last night and if she should get a lawyer for her brother.

"Sure I will take you. Nick, do you and Erica want a ride to your car first or do you want to stay here and we will come back here after we are done at the police station?"

Nick answered, "No you two go ahead, we will stay here for a while and if we do decide to go we can get a cab to take us to our car."

Angie and Tom left and Erica and Nick went to the cafeteria for a cup of coffee and a sandwich.

Erica sipped her coffee and said, "Boy I needed this. We got up at what, 5:00 am this morning and it has been one heck of a day. Sure didn't turn out like we planned."

Nick interrupted Erica, "Look at that man over there. I just saw him counting his change and looking at the prices of the donuts. He doesn't look like he has much money. I'll be right back." Nick got up and went over to the man. Erica could see him talking to him for a few minutes and then they stood in line and got some food and the man came walking over to the table with Nick.

"This is my wife Erica." Nick introduced.

The man sat down and said, "Mam I can't thank you enough. I have been here since last night. My wife had a heart attack and I haven't had a thing to eat since lunch yesterday. I rushed out of the house so fast to get here when I got the call that my wife had a heart attack, that I forgot my wallet."

"Is your wife going to be all right?" Erica asked.

"Yes they had to put in a stent. They said she will be fine, but I just don't want to go home and leave her here alone. She was pretty scared. If you give me your address I will sent some money to pay you kids back."

"That is not necessary." Nick smiled. "We are glad we could help. I hope your wife has a full recovery."

As they walked up the hall to the waiting room outside Winnie's room Erica said, "Well we got to buy a hungry person food today after all."

Nick smiled. They sat down and waited for a while, not knowing if they should just go on home or if they should wait to talk more to Michael and his son and his son's wife. They weren't sure if Angie and Tom were going to come back to the hospital after the police station. So they just sat and looked at magazines. After sitting there for about forty-five minutes, Michael came out of the room and sat down next to Nick. He said, "Winnie is still not responding. The doctor had some good news that her blood pressure and pulse are coming up, so that's good. I just want to give Bill and Judy some time alone with her."

Then he looked right into Nick's eyes and asked him to explain to him exactly what led up to this day. He said, "Your friend Angie said that my

A

mom asked you two to go find her and apologize to her because she fired her years ago and then to find that other guy that was with her and apologize to him for something and then she wanted the four of you to go feed hungry people in Chicago with her money. I just don't get it and where did she get the money?"

Nick started to say something but Michael squinted his eyes and said, "And it just happened that this Angie girls brother had my Winnie tied up in a trailer. I am starting to think there is more to this story. In fact I am calling the police." Then he looked into Nicks eyes with a hateful stare and said, "I am not stupid, you all kidnapped Winnie. You tied her up in that old trailer and you probably threatened my old mother that if she said anything and didn't give you money, you would kill Winnie. That is why she gave you guys that jewelry isn't it?"

Erica and Nick were shocked. They had no idea that he was thinking this way. Erica tried to explain how it all really happened but he interrupted and said, "You can tell that to the police and you better get a good lawyer."

Nick said, "Please just give us five minutes to explain the whole story and you will understand."

"I don't want to hear your cacamainy story. It is so obvious you all took advantage of my mother. I put her in that care center because I was afraid someone would take advantage of her if she were on her own at her age and then someone who works at the care center does it. You two make me sick" He yelled at the top of his lungs.

A

Erica kept trying to say please but Nick said, "Let's just go." Everyone in the waiting room was staring at them as they tried to leave. Then Bill came out of Winnie's room and said, "Wait a minute, what's all of the yelling? I want to talk to you two about what happened to my little girl."

Michael was seething with hatred, "These two kidnaped her that is what happened and they got mom's jewelry that belonged to Bet Midler for the ransom."

"Is this true?" Bill asked in a cracking voice, and he started to cry. His wife came out of the room and was wondering what was going on.

Nick said, "Please can we all sit down and we can explain to you everything that happened leading up to us finding Winnie. Then you can call your mother and she will tell you the exact thing. Then you can ask Angie and Tom and they will say the same thing."

"That is because you all rehearsed this story." Michael was still seething.

"Your mom will have no reason to go along with a story anymore because you have Winnie and she loves that girl so much. Don't you think she would tell the truth now if we had done this to Winnie?" Nick argued.

Winnie's mother Judy spoke up, "Please let's all sit down and let them tell us what happened."

Everyone in the waiting room was staring at them all so Judy asked a nurse if there was a quit place they could go to talk. The nurse showed them all to a room that had a big round table with several chairs around it

A

and she told them that they could use this room. They all went into the room and sat down. The nurse said, "There is a coffee pot on the counter if you want you can make yourselves a pot of coffee." Judy thanked her and shut the door and they all sat down.

Erica started at the very beginning. She told them why she took the job and how Trudy had no friends there and she was trying to get to know her and get her to socialize a little because that is what she was hired to do. Then one day Trudy opened up to her and told her how she was not proud of some of the things she had done in the past and that she had been talking to the preacher at Sunset and he told her all she had to do was ask forgiveness and she said that she did ask God to forgive her but she wanted to do more. She asked us to go find some people and bring them to her so she could apologize and give them all a gift. So we did. When Erica told them about Angie and how their mother fired her and about the reason why they all said that sounds like something she would do. Then Erica told them that Angie was still bitter after all of these years and blamed Trudy for the fact that she never went to college and was never able to help her sister who died from a drug overdose and her little brother who had a drug problem. She wanted to be a financial adviser like Trudy and make a lot of money and help her family but it never happened and she blamed Trudy.

Then Erica told them the reason she wanted to apologize to Tom they were all in shock. They never knew that that their father and grandfather had cheated on Trudy. Erica felt a little bit bad about telling them. She hoped Trudy wouldn't be mad at her but she felt she had to tell the whole truth because she didn't want to be arrested for kidnapping. A

Then she told them about Arleen and they all said, "AWW"

When she got to the part about digging up the grave she decided she better be truthful about the money and coins even though Trudy had told her when Michael found out about the jewelry not to tell him about the money or coins. She told them that Trudy gave them each $20,000 and she said, "We paid off our cars with our $20,000 but if you want the money back we will refinance and give it back to you and we still have the rest of the money hidden in our house. When we found out how valuable that the jewels were we buried them in our back yard. We planned to leave them there until Michael was ready to help us sell them for Trudy."

Then she told them about the little boy named Jason and how Trudy wanted to set up a college fund for him and how after they met him they decided to try and adopt him and that she has already started the paper work but with Nick being arrested the other day because of the jewelry and if they get blamed for kidnapping then the adoption is not going to be able to happen.

She sighed and went on and told them about how Trudy wanted them to go to Chicago and buy hungry people meals because when she was younger she cussed out the people on the streets who asked for money and told them to get a job. Michael actually laughed and said, "That's my mom."

Then Erica said, "So this morning when we got to Angie's house to pick her up to go to Chicago for the weekend just as we were getting in the car to leave she got the call from her brother that he was in jail and needed her help. She wanted us to all go on and go to Chicago without

A

her but we all said no way. Then we were in the car getting ready to go take Angie to the police station to find out more information about what happened with her brother and Nick asked her what her brother said to her about an old modular home."

Nick interrupted his wife and said, "Well when Angie got the phone call from her brother I heard her say what modular home? So I ask her what that was about and she said he told her to go check an old abandoned modular home and so I said lets go check it. Angie thought he probably just had drugs hidden in it or maybe some weed growing in it and she said she didn't care about that right now she just wanted to get to the police station. But I insisted we go check it out first so we did and that is when we found Winnie."

"Oh my God! If you hadn't insisted she wouldn't be alive. The doctor said she couldn't have held on much longer without fluids." Judy got out of her chair and went over and hugged Nick.

"So you believe this story?" Michael asked his daughter in law.

"Yes I do and I believe God had his hand in all of this. It is a miracle. We have all been praying for a miracle and we got a miracle. In a sense Grandma Trudy saved Winnie's life. She was trying to do something good to make up for her past wrongs and because of it, Winnie is alive." Judy said with tears running down her cheeks. There wasn't a dry eye in the room.

The nurse tapped on the door and opened it up and said, "Winnie is out of the coma.

A

They all jumped up and quickly made their way to her room. Erica and Nick waited in the waiting room right outside of Winnie's room to give the family privacy.

"I hope she is alright. The doctor said something earlier about her possibly having brain damage." Nick grabbed Erica's hand. "Let's say a prayer that she doesn't have brain damage."

Erica never heard Nick pray out loud before. He said a beautiful prayer asking God to please let Winnie have a total recovery. They both sat in silence for a moment. Erica looked over at Nick and he had his eyes closed and his hands folded.

When he opened his eyes, he looked over at Erica and said, "I love you."

"I love you too." She smiled and squeezed his hand.

Then they started talking about how this morning when they left the house they were planning to have a fun weekend getaway in Chicago and never dreamed that they would spend the day in a hospital and possibly end up getting arrested for kidnapping.

Angie and Tom came back to the hospital after they were finished at the police station. Erica told them that Winnie woke up and the family is in there right now. Then she told them that Michael thought that the four of them kidnapped Winnie and set this whole thing up to get that jewelry from Trudy.

"Oh no, do they really think that?" Angie was so emotionally drained

A

she could hardy talk.

"Well, we told them the whole story and I think they believe us. At least they haven't had us arrested yet. What did you find out at the police station?" Erica asked.

"They said that my brother did try to rob a store and he shot and killed the clerk and left the scene. They picked him up down the road and he still had the weapon on him and the store has it all on video so it is pretty much cut and dry." She was shaking and so visibly upset. Tom had his arm around her the whole times she was talking. "They said he had heroin and alcohol in his system. So he has drug charges, murder charges, and now kidnapping charges against him." She started to cry harder, "They wouldn't let me see him. How did my little brother turn out to be such a horrible person? He is a monster."

"Drugs Angie, you said he has been using since he was like 13. Drugs will mess you up." Nick didn't know what else to say. "Let's just hope Winnie is alright."

Erica's phone started ringing, "It's Trudy, and I'm not going to answer it. I want to wait and find out how Winnie is before I talk to her." She walked over to the nurse's station to see if they could tell her if Winnie had any brain damage. The nurse said the doctor is in there right now. All I know is she is conscious."

Finally Michael came out of the room. He walked over and sat down by Angie. "She is awake and it doesn't appear that there is any brain damage. She is very week and could only get out a few sentences. She

A

said she had a flat tire and a guy stopped to help her. Instead of helping he forced her in his car and took her somewhere and raped her and handcuffed her and she thinks he gave her drugs." Then he looked at Angie and said, "I guess it was your brother who did this to her."

Angie started crying and apologizing. Michael told her she wasn't responsible for what her brother does. Then he rubbed his chin and said, "It still seems like such a coincidence that you all got money from my mom and then Winnie is found. If you four did have something to do with this you will be sorry. If you held Winnie for ransom and told my mom not to tell anyone but to give you money and you will let her go, I will find out about it and you will wish you were never born."

"You just said that Winnie said a guy kidnapped her. So Tom and I can go in there right now and you can ask her if she has ever seen either one of us before?" Nick stood up and motioned for Tom to come with him.

"Yes, the guy was this girl's brother. Of course you wouldn't do it yourselves." Michael shook his head.

Angie had about all she could take for one day and she let him have it. "So you think I had my brother kidnap her so I could get money and then just let my brother take the rap. My brother, my only living relative is in jail probably for life. Your great granddaughter is in that room fighting for her life and you are sitting here accusing us. Let me tell you something, this couple right here that you are threatening, they have been nothing but caring and helpful to your mother and it is because of them that your great granddaughter is even alive." She looked over at

A

Tom, "Will you please take me home."

Tom and Angie got up to go, "Do you guys want to go? I'll give you a ride to your car." Tom said looking at Erica and Nick. They all got up and left. When they got in the car Tom suggested that they all stay the night at his house. He said he didn't want Angie to be alone tonight and it has been such a long day he didn't think Nick and Erica should drive all the way home. Tom pulled into the McDonalds where he worked and told them all to wait in the car for a minute he was going to grab some food for them all. While they were sitting in the car Erica's phone rang. "I don't recognize this phone number. I guess I better answer maybe it is Michael calling to apologize." She put it on speaker phone and answered. "Hello."

The voice on the other side said, "Hi Erica, my daughter c-called S-sunset c-care center and got the price information. Sh-she said that if I s-s-sell my h-house and with my s-savings and the money f-f-from Trudy I might be able to live th-there for a year or ma-maybe t-two. Then I might h-h-have to move t-to a cheaper p-place."

"That's great news Arleen did your daughter put your name on the waiting list at Sunset?"

"Not yet, I have t-to s-sell my house f-f-first."

"Well when I go to work on Monday I am going to put you on the waiting list so that if your house does sell fast maybe they can get you in. If your house doesn't sell and your name comes up they will just keep your name on the list for the next opening."

"Thanks Erica, I'm s-so excited. I know I will l-l-love living there."

A

"It would be wonderful to have you there. I have to go now but I will call you soon. Bye now."

Tom came back out and got in the car with several bags of food. "Are you planning on seeing some hungry people on the streets and feeding them or something?" Nick joked.

"This is some food for us." Tom didn't get the joke.

"It looks like enough to feed the homeless." They all laughed.

After they all ate a bunch of hamburgers and french-fries and chocolate shakes they collapsed in Tom's living room. Angie was exhausted. She sat in the recliner and Tom stood behind it and rubbed her shoulders.

Erica's phone rang again. "Now what does Arleen want." She answered the phone. "Oh hi Trudy, did you hear the news that Winnie is conscious and talking?" Erica sat quit listening for what seemed like five minutes. Then she said, "Thanks for calling Trudy, I'll talk to you tomorrow."

She hung up the phone and told the others what Trudy said, "Her son called her and asked her if we were the ones who took Winnie and made her keep quit and give us the jewels and money if she wanted to ever see Winnie again. Trudy said she told him that was not what happened. She said she told him what happened is that his pushing Winnie to go to college when she didn't want too and him being so damn controlling caused Winnie to run away. And something bad happened to her. But because of a lot of prayers, God sent these lovely people into our

A

lives who found Winnie and got her to a hospital. Then she told him he better quit being so suspicious of everyone or he is going to end up just like her. In a nursing home wishing he could go back in time and change the mean things he did."

They all cheered.

"Way to go Trudy." Angie perked up a little.

Chapter sixteen

They all fell asleep early and Nick and Erica left in the morning. They offered to give Angie a ride home but Tom said he would take her home later.

They stopped by the hospital to see how Winnie was doing before they headed home. Her parents were there in the room with her. They had spent the night but Michael had gone home last night. Nick and Erica were glad they didn't have to see him. Bill and Judy were very kind to them and thanked them over and over for finding her and getting her to a hospital. They apologized for Michael's behavior. "He is a lot like Grandma, suspicious of everyone. I think it is awesome what you guys did for my Granny. She has always been tight with her money and afraid to get close to anyone because she was always thinking everyone only liked her because of her money. So the fact that she is giving money away and trusting people makes me really happy. She is softening up in her old age." Bill said with a smile.

Erica replied, "I think the preacher at Sunset had a lot to do with it."

Bill said, "I think you had a lot to do with it." He squeezed Erica's hand. Then he looked over at his little girl lying in the bed sleeping. "And because of it, her life was saved."

Nick asked, "How is she doing?"

"The doctor says she will make a full recovery, besides some emotional scars. She was so dehydrated but they have pumped a lot of fluids and nutrients into her and they said if she is up to it she will be able

A

to try to eat some food this afternoon."

"Have you told Trudy the good news?" Erica asked.

"I haven't talked to her but I am sure my dad has called her."

Well I will see her tomorrow at work and I will make sure she knows not to worry, that Winnie is going to be fine. She told me that Winnie is her favorite."

Bill smiled, "I think everyone knows that. Thank you guys and I apologize again for my dad. Please tell Angie that we are just so thankful that Winnie is ok and we know she is not responsible for what her brother did."

"I will tell her that will mean a lot to her. She is feeling awful about all of this." Erica hugged Bill and Judy and said good bye and they headed out to their car to go home.

It was a busy week for Erica. The adoption people called and set up a night to come and see where they live and talk with them about the process. Then one night a counselor came over to talk to them about the challenges they will have with Jason because of the tragedy of losing his whole family. Then another counselor came over and introduced herself she would be Jason's counselor if he is placed with them. Her name was Mary Jo and she only lived a few streets over. She said she will need to come over and talk with Jason and them at least three times a week at first.

A

Arleen was calling Erica about every other day talking about how excited she is and that she is having her house painted and then she will put it up for sale. Erica put her name on the waiting list at work. Ada still wasn't back to Sunset and things weren't looking good for her. Erica decided she would go on the weekend to the hospital to visit her.

Besides all of that, Michael called Erica and left a message that he wanted to meet with her and Nick sometime soon. She hoped it was to apologize and not to accuse them of kidnapping or stealing an old lady's money. Nick said he probably is going to ask them to give the jewelry back to him. Erica figured Nick was probably right but for now let's just keep it buried.

One good thing about the week was that the gal's in C were getting along better than ever. They all decided they were going to start participating in the water aerobics that Sunset offered and they were still making it an every afternoon thing to all play Julies grandma's game. They all bet a dollar a game and everyone was really enjoying playing it. Even the gal's in room 7 and 8 joined them for grandma's game and an occasional karaoke party.

The director of Sunset care center called Erica in her office and told her she was doing such a good job making life a little better for the girls in her section and then she gave her a raise. She told her that is our main goal for everyone to be happy here. "Before you started we took a poll of everyone in Sunset. They were to grade on a scale of one to ten how satisfied they were with living here. The average score in all of the categories in section C was 6 just before you started working here. We

A

took the poll again this week and section C's average was 9. It was the highest score in the whole facility. Our goal is for our resident's family to feel good about leaving their loved one here in our care. They pay a lot of money for them to be here and they expect better that a 6 on a scale to 10 for their happiness." Then she told Erica, next quarter when they take the poll if she can get a 10 from section C Erica will be getting an even better raise. They have never got an average score of 10 from any of the sections and to get a 10 in all of the areas is their goal.

By the end of the week Winnie was doing great and was able to leave the hospital and go home. She told her parents that she is just going to take one semester off college and then start back up next semester but she wants to change her major to finance because she wants to be just like her Granny. When Trudy heard that she was thrilled.

Erica and Nick met with Michael one evening and it turned out he just wanted to apologize for accusing them of kidnapping. He also gave them a piece of paper with an estimate for the jewelry that his dad had gotten years ago. He told them it should be worth even more than this now. Then he gave them a card for a jeweler that he knows that will give them a fair price. He told them to sell it and spend the money however his mom wants it spent. He told them that he trust them. When they told him that it was still buried in their back yard he laughed. Everything seemed to be working out.

Jason came to live with Erica and Nick the last week of August. They were just his foster parents for now but they already had the adoption process started. Erica was able to take two weeks off work to be with him

A

before school started. They were hoping with a lot of counseling he would be ready to go to school when it starts in two weeks.

It turned out Mary Jo (his counselor) had a son in the same grade as Jason. She brought him over one day and they really hit it off. They were down the basement playing Nintendo and ping pong all day. Having a friend was going to make it a lot easier for Jason to go to school when it starts.

Mary Jo offered to take Jason to school and pick him up after school, because she always drives her son Ben any way. They would get home about 45 minutes before Erica so she said she would just take Jason to her house and Erica could pick him up there when she gets off work. Mary Jo makes her own schedule so she never schedule's any appointments from three till five. Her husband gets home from work at five and she sometimes works evenings after he gets home. They made a deal that if she ever needs to make an appointment between 4 and 5 Erica will watch the boys while she goes. Everything was working out great.

Jason's dog Buster came to live with them too. So now they had an eight year old boy and a dog. The dog was really a pretty good dog. It was house broken and it followed Jason everywhere he went. Having the dog with him helped Jason to adjust to his new home pretty quickly.

Tom and Angie stopped by Erica and Nick's house one Saturday morning. Erica answered the door and was so surprised to see them. "We have big news!" Angie couldn't contain her excitement.

Erica thought she was going to say they got engaged but she had a

A

wedding band on and she said we got married yesterday. "Tom proposed to me last weekend, and of course I said yes. We talked about it and we both decided we didn't want a wedding and we didn't want to wait."

Erica could hardly believe it. "Why didn't you call and tell me he proposed?"

"We were going to call and ask you two to be there at the court house with us but you have made a lot of long trips lately and with your new little boy we didn't want you to feel like you had to be there. Where is he anyway?"

"He is downstairs watching cartoons. I'll be right back." She said as she was already half way down the stair.

She came up the stairs with Jason but Buster about knocked them both over to get up the stairs and smell Tom and Angie.

"This is Buster and this is Jason." Erica put her hand on Jason's shoulder.

"So nice to meet you Jason," Tom shook his hand.

"Hi Jason, I am Angie. You sure have a cute dog."

Jason started hugging his dog. Erica could tell that he was feeling a little overwhelmed so she told him he could go back down stairs and watch cartoons if he wanted. Jason didn't say a word he just headed right back down the steps and Buster followed.

"He is still a little shy about meeting people." Erica explained.

A

"OH, I totally understand. The little guy just went through an awful ordeal. I'm so happy you guys found him. I know he will be OK now that he has you." Angie said and then looked over at her new husband. "Me married and you a mom all in a weeks' time.

"So you got married yesterday and you drove down here just to tell us?" Nick questioned.

"We are going to Kentucky Lake for our honeymoon. We're going to spend a week on a house boat. We wanted to tell you guys in person." Angie hugged Erica.

"I am so happy for you guys. Hey, do you have time to go to the Care Center and tell Trudy?" Erica said excitedly. "She is responsible for you guys meeting."

"We were talking about that in the car. We have the house boat reserved and can't pick it up until 2:00. What time is it?

"It's only ten" Erica looked at her watch.

Tom said, "We still have a three hour drive to get there but we don't have to be there at 2:00 on the nose or anything. I think we should go tell Trudy in person."

"Can we come? I want to see the look on Trudy's face when you tell her. Besides she hasn't met Jason yet." Erica started looking for her shoes.

"Honey, if we go and bring Jason it will take away from their news. Also it might be too much for Jason. You saw how shy he was when Angie tried to talk to him." Nick sat down on the couch. Angie went and sat

A

down by him.

"I want you guys to be there when we tell her. She did bring us together but so did you guys. If you guys didn't agree to help Trudy, then I would have never met Tom." Angie hugged Nick.

"Anyway, I think it would be cool for her to hear this news and to meet Jason at the same time, unless you don't think Jason is up to it."

Nick looked over at Erica sitting on the floor tying her shoes. "What do you think?"

"I want to go, let me go down and talk to Jason. I'm gonna ask him if he would like to go." Erica jotted down the stairs.

A few minutes later she came up the stairs with Jason. "He says he wants to go.

They drove separate so Tom and Angie could leave strait from the Care Center to get on the interstate and head to Kentucky for their honeymoon. When they got there they decided that Nick and Erica would go in first and introduce Jason to Trudy. Tom and Angie would wait about five minutes and then come in with their big announcement.

When Nick and Erica walked in with Jason, Trudy was laying on her couch watching TV. She jumped up faster than Erica has ever seen her move. She practically ran to Jason. She just started showering him with love. Erica thought that it was going to be too much for him but he was actually smiling and talking to her.

Then the door opened and Tom and Angie walked in and yelled

"Surprise." Angie was glowing with the biggest smile and she didn't have to say a word. She just pointed to her ring. Trudy screamed with excitement. They all walked over and sat down in Trudy's living room area. Trudy sat down in one recliner and Tom and Angie sat in the other recliner, Angie on his lap. Nick and Erica sat on the couch and Nick patted the couch for Jason to come over and sit by him, but Jason walked over and climbed up on Trudy's lap. Nick and Erica looked at each other in amazement.

They all sat and talked for a while. Angie told them all about the proposal and the courthouse wedding and about the adorable house boat they were renting for the week. Then the newlyweds said we got to go start our honeymoon. After the newlyweds left Trudy got up and took Jason over to the table and gave him a piece of paper and some crayons. The two of them started coloring pictures together.

Erica whispered to Nick, "Where in the world did she get crayons?"

They sat on the couch and watched Trudy and Jason color and talk and laugh.

They heard Jason say, "This is a picture of my dog. His name is Buster. Then he said, "This is a picture of what my house looked like before it burnded down.

Trudy gave him a little squeeze, "That's a nice house. You are really good at drawing."

"I know." Jason replied. Then Trudy gave him another squeeze.

A

"OK we got to get going big guy. I have a lot to get done today. I want to get the lawn mowed hopefully for the last time this season." Nick said as he was helping put the crayons back in the box.

"I want to stay here. Can I please?" Jason climbed up on Trudy's lap.

Erica and Nick didn't know what to think. He really liked Trudy and was really opening up to her. Erica couldn't wait to tell his counselor Mary Jo about this and see what she says.

She told him that they had to go now but Erica promised Jason that she would bring him to see Miss. Trudy again soon. Jason asked if he could bring Buster next time they came. Erica said that she thought that would be a good idea. She guessed it would be OK because Betty's grandson brings his dog to the Care Center every once in a while and all of the old people loved it.

Trudy squeezed Jason one last time and said to him, "I can't wait for you to come back and bring Buster. I am looking forward to meeting him."

Jason hugged her tight and said, "I can't wait too."

With all that was going on Erica never did get a chance to go see Ada in the hospital. Her family moved her things out of Sunset. They said that if she does get out of the hospital they were going to move her in with her daughter. When her family was at the Care Center getting her things Erica gave them a card to give to her and asked if she could come see her at her daughter's house when she gets to feeling better and they said of course. Erica gave Ada's daughter her phone number.

A

Arleen's house sold fast and Erica was able to pull some strings and she was going to be able to move into Ada's room.

The following weekend Arleen's daughter moved all of her stuff into Ada's old room and on that Monday Arleen moved in. She absolutely loved it there. She got along with all of everyone in section C right off the bat.

She didn't waste any time, she joined the aerobics class and she learned the dice game. She never missed an opportunity to sing karaoke.

So Arleen played the dice game every afternoon. She seemed to win most of the time. She had a huge stash of dollar bills in her room. She really loved the karaoke party's because when she sang she didn't stutter. Everyone made a big deal over her voice and she loved the attention.

Arleen wasn't too happy when she heard that Angie married Tom. "Just w-w-wait t-till I see her. I am g-g-onna let her have it f-for s-stealing m-my man."

Erica told her with all of the good looking men here in the Care Center you will forget about Tom in no time. Arleen was always in a good mood, enjoying every day at Sunset. She always brightened up everyone's day. Erica was so glad to have her in her section.

A

Chapter seventeen

Angie's brother had his trial and it looked like he would be spending the rest of his life in jail. Angie decided not to spend Trudy's money on a lawyer because she talked to a lawyer that Tom knew and he said you will be throwing your money away. It's an open and shut case. Even the best attorney won't be able to keep him from prison. She felt really bad for a while about not even trying to help him but she and Tom went to visit him in prison a few times and he was doing really well. A preacher had been talking to him in prison and he said he has asked for forgiveness and ask the lord in his heart and he was off drugs and going to bible studies. Angie said that he looked better than he has looked in years.

That fall they all finally took a weekend trip to Chicago and spent a thousand dollars buying hungry people on the streets dinner. They just walked down Michigan Boulevard and looked in the shops and had a great time. Whenever anyone asked for a hand out they would say are you hungry? If they said yes they would go to the nearest restaurant and get them a table and they would tell them to order whatever they wanted. Then they would ask the server the total for their bill and add a very nice tip and ask her to take super good care of them and then they would leave and wait for someone else who needed lunch.

Jason went along and he was very compassionate. The whole experience was really good for him. One of the homeless men had a little boy with him that was about Jason's age. When they took them in the restaurant and told them they could order whatever they wanted. The little boy got so excited. He could not decide what to order. The dad told

A

the little boy to hurry up because the waitress was waiting. So Jason climbed in the booth and helped the little boy pick something out and then he said you might as well go ahead and order some chocolate cake too. The little boy's eyes lit up and he said, "Can I?"

Nick said, "Of course you can." He told the waitress to add two pieces of chocolate cake and to bring him the bill. They paid for the food and left a big tip and when they were leaving, Jason ran back and gave the little boy a hug.

Jason said when he grows up he wants to work hard and make a lot of money so he can go to Chicago regularly and buy dinners for people and volunteer at a homeless shelter. They visited a shelter while they were there and donated five thousand dollars of Trudy's money.

They all really had a good time in Chicago. They stayed in a hotel that had bikes for their guest to use for free. So Saturday evening they all took a bike ride along the beach. It was a beautiful crisp cool night. Someone was setting off fireworks. They all sat on the beach and watched fireworks and ate hot dogs from a vender.

As they sat on the beach and watched the fireworks Jason played in the sand. Then he came over to Erica and said, "I am having the best day ever!" Then he went back to building a sand castle with another little boy he had met at the beach.

Angie smiled at Erica and squeezed her hand. The four of them where becoming best of friends.

After that weekend Jason started to warm up to Angie, but nothing

A

like he did with Miss Trudy. Mary Jo said that probably Miss Trudy reminded him of his real grandma. So Erica took him to see his real grandparents in the nursing home in St. Louis. They were really old and in such poor health that they really didn't interact with him very much. So she brought Jason to see Trudy whenever she could. Sometimes Buster would come along. Everyone loved Buster. He would do all of his tricks and everyone would clap. So Jason started teaching his dog more and more new tricks. Pretty soon he had a whole routine. Even residents from the other sections would come over to section C when Jason and Buster were there to watch Jason show off Busters tricks.

They got the trust fund for Jason's college set up. It was for twenty thousand dollars for college and if Jason did not go to college Erica and Nick would get the money. Trudy also gave Angie and Tom a very generous wedding gift. Trudy asked Erica to send some money to a couple of charities. When the cash was all gone, they dug up the jewelry and took it to the guy Michael suggested. They received almost three hundred thousand dollars for it and the coins. They opened a checking account in Trudy and Erica's name and put all of the money in it. Then every time Trudy wanted to give money away she would write a check and ask Erica to do some crazy thing like one time they all had to go find a girl that Trudy beat up on the playground when she was Six. The women didn't even remember getting beat up but she was grateful for the money anyway.

One time she asked Erica to try and find a guy that had backed into her car about 12 years ago. He didn't have insurance and he said he didn't have any money to pay her. So Trudy took him to court and they

A

garnished his wages. She said at the time she was thinking he needed to learn a lesson that you can't just go around without having insurance and still drive.

She told Erica that he begged her not to take him to court and let him pay just a little every month because he had two little kids and he was struggling to make it and she said no way. Now she was feeling really bad about it but she didn't remember his name or anything.

Erica had to call Michael and ask him if he could find out who the guy was. She was worried that he was going to say that his mother was being ridicules and he might start asking about all the other money she has given away. But he was really nice on the phone and he said he would do some digging in his mother's files and get back with her. He said he was planning to come see her soon and he would let me know when he comes.

A couple of days later he came to Sunset for a visit when he got there he couldn't believe it his mom was in Julie's room singing and having a ball. He was thrilled to see his mom getting along with everyone and having such a good time.

When Erica saw him standing in the door way watching his mom sing, she walked over to him.

"I have the information you asked about. I would like to go with you to give the money to this guy. Would you mind?"

"Of course not, but usually your mom wants them to come here so she can apologize in person and then give them the money." Erica
A

explained.

"OK I have a phone number. I will call him and tell him what my mother wants to do and I will try to be here when he comes."

Just then Trudy noticed him standing in the door way talking to Erica and she motioned for him to come over and sing with her. Michael told them that he would rather just listen to them sing but Julie insisted that he pick out a song and sing. He looked through Julie's book of songs and picked out the song 'against all odds' by Barry Manilow. "Look mom, here is one of your favorite songs."

Michael and Trudy sang it together. They sounded pretty good and Michael ended up picking out a couple more songs to sing. He stayed at the Care Center for about two hours that day. He was actually having a good time.

Michael called Erica the next day and said he got a hold of the guy who backed into his mom's car 12 years ago and told him the good news that his mom was sorry for not being understanding and that she wanted to give him the money back. "He was so thrilled. He said actually he is still struggling to get by and that money would really help. Then he said he shouldn't have been driving without insurance and that my mom had every right to take him to court. But he is going to come to Sunset Care Center tomorrow morning and I am going to try to be there."

When Erica hung up the phone she told Nick that she thinks Michael is starting to change. His mom's new attitude is rubbing off on him.

The next day the young man came to see Trudy and Michael was

A

there waiting and welcomed him in the room. They sat down and Trudy apologized. "I was such a bitch."

The guy laughed and said, "If I was driving a beautiful Mercedes and someone without insurance backed into it I would be a bitch too." They all laughed. "I have insurance now and I have had it ever since then. You taught me an important lesson."

Trudy said, "I'm glad you learned a lesson. Everyone should have auto insurance it is a law. But I remember that you said you had two little children and you were struggling and I was so mean to not just let you make payments instead of having your wages garnished."

"It was really tough but we made it through. My little girls are teenagers now. I have raised them on my own and times are still tough but we manage and we have insurance."

Trudy got out her check book and started writing a check and handed it to him.

"Twenty thousand dollars! Are you kidding? I think it was about three thousand I paid you to fix your Mercedes."

Erica saw Michael's look on his face when he heard how much she gave him and he looked like he was going to flip his lid. But he remained calm and didn't say anything until the man left. Then he said, "MOTHER why did you give him so much?"

"You heard him. He is raising two teenagers by himself. That's not easy even when you have a lot of money try to imagine doing it when you are broke."

Michael grabbed his mom's hand. "I am really proud of you mom. You have changed so much and I want to be a better person because of you." Erica left the room to give them some time alone.

Around Christmas time Angie and Tom moved down close to Nick and Erica. Tom was able to transfer to the McDonalds right near Nick and Erica's house. Angie quit her job at the hotel. She applied for a job at Sunset and they hired her to be part of the cleaning crew and she would be able to start in January. They bought a house in the same subdivision as Nick and Erica. It was close enough that they could walk to each other's houses.

Jason was doing really well in school. He had days when he would dwell on what happened and not be able to shake it. Since Mary Jo just lived a few streets over she would come talk to him and she always knew just what to say. He and Ben were best friends and having a good friend like that really helped him a lot.

Nick and Erica turned out to be really good at being parents. Nick spent a lot of time out in the yard with Jason playing catch, in the basement playing Nintendo, or in the garage working on things. The three of them would have ping pong tournaments on Friday night in the basement. Erica would usually win. Except when Tom and Angie would come over and join the tournaments, then Tom was usually the champ. Jason loved it when Tom and Angie came over because they would always bring him some McDonalds.

A

The adoption process was moving right along. They were told that they would probably be Jason's legal parents in about a year. Then one day they got a call that Jason's aunt wanted to try to get custody. Apparently she heard about the college trust fund and was calling the agency and asking a lot of questions about the money. It really made Erica mad because she hadn't come to see him or even call to see how he was doing until she heard about the money.

The women from the agency who was handling the case told Erica that because she is his biological family. The court will probably award her custody. Erica and Nick were devastated.

Then one day Trudy got a call from Jason's aunt. She told her who she was and thanked Trudy for setting up a trust fund for her little nephew. She said she hasn't been able to stop thinking about little Jason ever since her sister died in that fire. She asked Trudy if there was some way she could get that trust fund money now so she could afford to come to Missouri and fight for custody of Jason because after all he belongs with family.

Trudy tried to remain calm and sound professional. "Absolutely not, that money is in a college trust fund. It cannot be touched until Jason is ready to go to college. In the event that he does not go to college it will go to the beneficiary. It was set up for Erica Probps to be the beneficiary and that cannot be changed even if she does not remain his legal guardian.

"You mean even if I legally adopt him the beneficiary will not be me? That is ridicules. I am his aunt." the voice on the phone sounded shocked.

A

Trudy could not remain calm any longer. "No mam it will not be you. I set up that trust fund for that little boy to go to college and you will never get a penny of that money no matter what you do."

The next evening, Erica got a call from the adoption agency. They told her that the aunt withdrew her application. When Nick got home from work she told him the news and they all hopped in the car to go tell Trudy the good news.

"Can I bring Buster?"

"Let's leave Buster here this time and we will stop and get some pizza to take with us and share with Trudy to celebrate.

"What are we celebrating?" Jason asked.

"We are celebrating because you are our little boy and we are so happy about it." Erica looked at him in the back seat and felt so much joy in her heart. She loved that little guy so much already.

"Does that mean you adopted me now?"

"Well the adoption isn't final yet but it is going to be and nobody can take you from us." She reached back and patted his leg.

He smiled at her and said, "I'm glad. I know my real mom would like you."

Erica literally felt a warm feeling all through her chest. She looked over at Nick and the look on his face said that he felt it too.

A

Chapter seventeen

Arleen was having a ball living at Sunset. The golden girls called her a golden girl want to be. She liked hanging out over in the men's section and flirting with the men as much as the golden girls did. Her daughter told Erica that she is only going to be able to live there for two years tops because her funds would run out. Her daughter said that she was just glad she will have two really great years and then she will either have to come live with her or go to a state ran nursing home.

Erica told Trudy what Arleen's daughter had said and Trudy pulled out a check and wrote it for enough for her to stay for two additional years. She said if Arleen is still healthy and wanting to live here after four years and if I still have some money left I will pay for her to stay longer.

Arleen's daughter couldn't believe it when she heard about it. She called Trudy a saint. Trudy laughed, "Now that's a first."

It was really great when Angie started working at Sunset. Erica got to see her off and on throughout the day. After being a maid at the hotel for such a long time she was really good at her job. You could always tell if Angie made a bed because it looked perfect and if the floors were extra shiny you knew Angie did it.

One day Angie was cleaning Trudy's bathroom when Winnie came to visit. Angie heard someone come into the room and she heard Trudy say Yippy my little Winnie is here. Angie started shaking and was afraid to come out of the bathroom. When she did come out she looked at Winnie

A

and started crying. She walked over to her and fell at her feet and cried. Winnie didn't know what was going on until Trudy told her who Angie was.

"You helped save my life. You don't need to apologize. I need to fall at your feet and thank you. Your brother hurt me, not you. You helped save me."

"But I feel reasonable for him." Angie cried.

"Well you are not. He did it and he is paying for it in prison so you need to stop feeling responsible." Winnie put her hand out and helped Angie up off the floor.

They talked for a while and Angie told her how her brother got off drugs in prison and how he found God and is going to bible study. "Actually he asked me to get your address for him so he could write you an apology letter but I wouldn't give it to him. I told him it might creep you out to get a letter from him."

Winnie said, "Ya, I don't know if I am ready for that. Maybe sometime in the future, but not now."

"I understand that is why I didn't give it to him." Angie said and started back to work.

Then Winnie said as she pulled out some papers from her purse, "Granny Trudy, I am here because I need your help picking out classes for the spring semester."

Angie had her back turned dusting the coffee table and she almost

A

screamed. She turned around and she saw Trudy staring at her. They both could hardly contain their selves. They both started laughing and carrying on. Winnie didn't know what to think. "It's a long story, but years ago Angie asked me for help picking out classes. I didn't help her but I am darn sure not going to make that mistake again." Trudy winked at Angie.

Angie left the room to give Winnie time with her Granny, but the conversation made her feel better.

When Winnie's classes started in the spring she started coming to Sunset quit often to do her homework with her Granny. There was a few times when Angie would be cleaning Trudy's room and the two of them would be doing homework. Trudy would be giving her Granddaughter advice and Angie would think that is what I wanted from her years ago. But instead of feeling bitter she felt a sense of joy. She was so thankful that Winnie was alive. She was so happy with her marriage and her new job and her new house and her new friends and everything turned out perfect. She realized it was not Trudy's fault that her brother got so messed up on drugs and did horrible things. Anyway her brother was doing great in prison. Perhaps better than he ever would have done in rehab on his own.

The beginning of June Erica and Nick officially became Jason's legal parents. The school year had ended and Jason had adjusted quit well. Mary Jo watched Jason during the summer days while Erica was at work. He and Ben were best friends so Jason loved going over there every day.

A

Erica and Nick had a bar b q on June 5th to celebrate the adoption. They invited Mary Jo, Ben, Tom and Angie. They grilled burgers and played volleyball in the back yard. Angie said to Erica, "I'm surprised you didn't ask Trudy to come."

"I really did think about it but then I would have needed to invite Arleen and then what about the rest of the lady's? I didn't want to leave anyone out and I wasn't sure what anyone's families would think about me taking them out of the Care Center."

"That's true, and I don't think any of them could play volleyball anyway."

"That's all I would need is for one of them to try to play and get hurt." Erica answered.

Angie laughed, "I know that Arleen would have tried to play."

Erica opened the cooler and grabbed a root beer. "Want one?"

"Yes, thank you." Angie pulled her lawn chair into the shade.

Jason came over to them as they were sitting under the shade tree drinking root beer. "Come on mom, we are going to play another game of volleyball. This time it will be girls against the boys." He grabbed Erica's hand and tried to pull her.

"That's not fair. There are four of you and only three of us." Angie yelled as she got up and headed toward the net.

Erica tapped Angie on the shoulder, "That's the first time he called me mom." She said with a tear in her eye.

"Girls serve first." Nick yelled as he threw the ball to Erica, who was still thinking about being called mom. The ball hit her in the head. Everyone laughed.

The guys won the first volleyball game by 15 points. So they gave the girls a ten point lead and played again. The guys beat the girls even with a ten point lead. Erica yelled I quit and went over to the shade and collapsed in a lawn chair. Angie and Mary Jo played one more game against Ben and Jason, while the men grilled the burgers. Mary Jo had brought a pan of baked beans and Angie had made potato salad. Erica had a big cake made and written on the cake was, 'Welcome to the family Jason!'

After everyone ate, Erica was getting ready to cut the cake, Nick yelled, "wait."

"I really feel like Trudy should be part of this celebration. Why don't we bring the cake up to Sunset and continue this celebration with her."

Mary Jo and Ben had other plans for the evening so they went on home and the rest of them all hopped in their cars and went to Sunset Care Center.

When they all walked in Trudy's room carrying a cake, Trudy was sitting at the table with Winnie helping her with homework.

Jason barged in and said, "We brought cake."

Erica explained that they were having a bar b q to celebrate the adoption being final and before they cut the cake they all felt like she should be there. "If it weren't for you Miss Trudy, we would have never even met Jason." Erica teared up and set the cake on the table and gave Trudy a hug.

"We were just about done with my homework anyway. I'm going to go ahead and go Granny." Winnie got up and started stacking her books.

"Can you please stay? It is awesome that you happened to be here. Look around the room. All of our lives have been changed because of your Granny." Nick took the books out of Winnie's hands and placed them on the counter. "We wouldn't have Jason, Tom and Angie wouldn't have each other. And you might not be alive. Let's make this a Thank You Trudy party!"

Erica said, "Your right Nick but before we cut the cake we need to go get Arleen. She needs to be part of this celebration too."

Erica went down the hall and found Arleen working on a crossword puzzle in her room. "Come on down to Trudy's room, we are having a party."

Arleen jumped right up and followed Erica down the hall to Trudy's room. When they walked in the room and Arleen saw that Tom was there she said, "Why didn't you tell me he was here? I would have fixed my hair and put on something pretty."

"Go find your own man and keep your hands off mine." Angie teased.

A

Nick whistled for everyone to be quit and then he gave a beautiful speech honoring Miss Trudy. He said everyone has things they would like to change about their past but not everyone does something about it. But because you decided to try to make up for some of the things that you had done that you weren't proud of, you changed lives. All of us in this room owe you a huge Thank you."

They cut the cake and everyone was eating cake and talking when Julie walked in and said, "I was looking for you Arleen. Are you guys having a party or what?"

Erica handed her a piece of cake and told her what they were celebrating and she talked them all into going to her little karaoke Christmas lounge and singing some songs.

"I have the perfect song for Trudy to sing." Julie said as she pulled out a CD and put it in the player and handed Trudy the microphone.

"What song is it?" Trudy asked. But Julie didn't answer she just started the song. It was a song by Eddie Money and the words say, "I want to go back, go back and do it all over."

Trudy agreed that the words were perfect and they played it a second time and everyone in the room sang. Even little Jason was singing at the top of his lungs.

While everyone was singing Erica looked around the room and thanked God for leading her to the job at Sunset Care Center. It literally changed her life.

A

They partied till late in the night. Singing songs and talking about all of the great things that have happened because of Miss Trudy. Then they all ate a little more cake and finally ended up going home at about midnight.

Monday when Erica got to work the receptionist told her that the director wanted to see her. As she walked down the hall to the director's office she was thinking that she was probably in trouble for having a party there on Friday night and staying so late. She thought, "Oh my gosh, we were pretty noisy."

Erica knocked on the office door. The director told her to come in and she pulled up a chair for Erica to sit down.

"Did you want to talk to me?" Erica said with a concerned look on her face.

"Oh don't worry; I just wanted to talk to you about our new quarterly polls we just got in. As you know our goal is for every section to score a ten. We haven't ever had even one section score a perfect ten in all categories for the entire eight years this Care Center has been open." She looked up from her papers with her glasses on the tip of her nose, "Until now!" Section C scored a ten in every category this quarter." She reached up and gave Erica a high five.

She scooted her chair over by Erica and showed her the results. "All sections scored better than last quarter. They went over all of the questions that were asked and over the answers that people gave and she showed Erica comments that some of her gal's had written. "Outstanding,

A

is all I can say. You have done an outstanding job and you will be getting the raise I told you about."

Erica left her office feeling really great. It was like this was what she was meant to do and to think she almost didn't take the job here.

On Friday night Erica called Angie to see if they were coming over for the usual Friday night ping pong tournament.

"Yes we will be a little late Tom is still at work. His relief called and said he would be late but we will be over later. Bye"

"See you later, bye sweetie."

They got there a little later than usual and Erica wanted to just sit and visit with her Friend Angie so she told the guys to go on and play ping pong without them.

Jason really wanted his mom and Angie to play in the ping pong tournament but they told him they wanted to just sit and talk, so it was just going to be the guys playing tonight. Tom chuckled as he went down the stairs, "What's wrong Jason are you scared to play against me without your mom."

Jason took off running down the steps "I want to play against Tom first OK dad."

He was calling Erica and Nick, mom and dad all of the time now. Angie noticed and asked, "Are you guys getting use being called mom and dad yet?"

A

"I'm still not use to it but I love it." Erica smiled.

The girls sat and chatted about work and about how much they like every one of the lady's at Sunset and about some of the funny things that the gals have done. They still couldn't get over how good everything in their lives has worked out thanks to Trudy.

"Will you guys come down and watch now?"

"We will be right down." Erica yelled because Jason was already half way back down the steps.

Erica and Angie got down stairs just in time to see Tom beat Nick 21 to 15. "OK so I play Tom. Are you ready to get beat by a nine year old?" Jason teased.

"This was the final game of the last tournament and if I beat Tom I'm the winner." Jason said excitedly.

Erica could tell Tom was easing up on Jason a little but Jason was actually pretty good. The game was tied 20 to20. Jason was getting so excited and he ended up winning 22 to 20. He marched around the basement saying I am the champion. "Hey next time I am at Sunset, I am going to ask Aunt Julie if she has the song that goes 'we are the champions we are the champions.' If she has that song I am going to sing it."

"Did you say Aunt Julie?" Erica asked.

"Yes she told me to call her that and Trudy said I could call her Granny. I love them. Can we go there tomorrow since it is Saturday?"

A

"Yes I guess I could take you up there tomorrow morning. I haven't taken you in a while. Want to come along Angie?"

"Sure I don't have any plans tomorrow."

"Can Buster come?"

"Yes Buster can come and show off his tricks."

"Oh boy! I'm going to go teach him a new trick right now." Jason ran up the steps with Buster following close behind.

"It's bed time in twenty minutes." Erica yelled.

"Let's get going honey. I have to work in the morning." Tom put his arm around Angie and they all went upstairs.

As they were walking out the door Jason yelled, "Bye Aunt Angie and Uncle Tom."

Before Jason had to go to bed he had already taught Buster a new trick. He showed his mom and dad. "Watch this, Buster give me a hug." Buster jumped up and put his paws on Jason's shoulders and put his face against Jason's neck and it really looked like he was giving him a hug.

Erica and Nick clapped and Jason gave Buster a treat. "All of the ladies are going to get a kick out of that trick. Now you need to go brush your teeth and go to bed now."

The next morning Erica Jason and Buster got in the car and went to pick up Angie and headed to the Care Center. Angie got in the car and said, "Are we crazy going to work on our day off?"

A

"Yes we are crazy, crazy about these ladies." Erica smiled.

When they got to Sunset Jason and Buster did their tricks for section C and then he went to all of the other sections to do his routine for everyone else. He was getting to be friends with all of the men in section A and B. He knew them all by name and they all just loved it when Jason and Buster came.

After he finished showing everyone his dog show they all hung out in Trudy's room for a while. There was a knock on the door and in walked the preacher. "Hello Miss Trudy. I see you have company. I will come back and visit tomorrow."

"No please stay." Trudy got up and went to the door and grabbed his hand and brought him over to sit down. "Everyone keeps saying that it is because of me that all of these things worked out so well but really it is because of this man."

The preacher sat down and asked what she was talking about. Trudy told him, "Talking to you on the weekends is what made me realize that I needed to change. I cannot thank you enough for helping me realize that."

Erica and Angie told the preacher the whole story about Trudy having money buried and about how she wanted to apologize to people from her past and about Winnie being found. They told him the whole long story of how all of their lives were changed because of this one lady repenting.

The preacher listened to the whole story and then he said, "When

A

you repent and tell the lord you are truly sorry for your sins, he forgives you and forgets the sins. You are washed clean. But sometimes we have a hard time forgetting them ourselves and sometimes we feel great regret for our past wrongs. Not too many people go to such great lengths to try to make things right. Trudy, would you mind if I put this whole story in my news letter this week?"

Trudy told the preacher she didn't mind and Erica and Angie spent the whole afternoon helping him write down all of the details while Jason and Trudy went down to Julies karaoke lounge to see if she had the song 'we are the champions.' Julie had the song and Jason marched around her room singing it at the top of his lungs.

The newsletter was published and Trudy started getting cards and letters from people saying how much she had inspired them.

Then one day Trudy got a visit from a lady who said she was an author and she wanted permission to use Trudy's story for a book. She said a percentage of the profits would go to her. Trudy gave her permission and the author visited everyone involved including Julie, Arleen and the golden girls. She took notes from everyone and it took about eight months but finally the book came out. It was titled 'Trudy's gift.'

The book sold thousands of copies. Every resident at Sunset bought one and Trudy autographed all of them. All of the proceeds that Trudy got went straight to a homeless shelter.

A

A

A

A

A

A

A

A

A

Made in the USA
Monee, IL
24 September 2021